TWIN MARINES IN HELL

From Grade School to Vietnam

Jerry Byrne

D1518311

Copyright © 2014 by Jerry Byrne

ISBN: 13- 978-1511727259

ISBN: 10-151172725X

3 4873 00508 0239

DEDICATION & THANKS

This book is especially dedicated to my twin brother John, who died of cancer on August 6, 2003 as a result of being exposed to Agent Orange, while serving with the Marine Corps in 1966. This herbicide was sprayed in the jungles of Vietnam during the war.

It is also dedicated to all my brothers from Kilo Company, Third Battalion, Seventh Marines, First Marine Division who died in country during the war. One more dedication goes to those who continue to battle the effects of Agent Orange years after the war.

There are many people I would like to thank for giving me encouragement in writing this book. Thanks to my wife Marie, for her support and reassurance. Thank you to my sons Christopher and Jerry, Ina, Jenoval and Jesavia for always being there for me. Thanks to all my family and friends for reading these stories and giving their input. For all those that I asked to read each chapter, thank you.

Semper Fi

TABLE OF CONTENTS

INTRODUCTION

After I retired from working 35 years in the elevator industry, I became more involved with various Veterans' Organizations. As part of their community outreach, I am asked to speak about my experiences in Vietnam to high school students. Teachers in these high schools think it is important for young people to hear about the military and Vietnam experience firsthand.

One day as I was speaking to the students about my experience, someone said, "You should put these memories on paper."

As I began to write them down, I was amazed to discover how many of my memories had been suppressed. As I started to write, a few pages turned into many.

This story is about my brother John and I growing up as children in Howard Beach and becoming men in the jungles of Vietnam. John died at the age of 58 from Agent Orange, a herbicide that was sprayed for years in South Vietnam.

Many times, I wish that he were here now to help me fill in the blank spots that I have forgotten.

THE DECEPTION

By Jerry Byrne

Mother and Father

Looked with disbelief

The telephone was ringing

Listen to me

But all was deaf

As the shades of evening

Darkened the room

I have told them before

That the day will come

That I joined the Marine Corps

The clocks stopped as if life ceased

Papers at my side

A rocket in motion

I advanced up the steps

Body was shaking

Breaking with sweat

Eyes in tears as I waved good-bye

The allegiance I pledged

Was to this great country of ours

Inhabiting my surrounding was

National pride

To all points of the compass

I will go

A soldier of fortune

Fighting in hell

When I got to P I

There was a surprise

I felt betrayed

Strangled and placed aside

A Marine Drill Instructor

Placed his eyes on mine

CHAPTER 1

THE TWINS

Two minutes after my brother John (nickname Jackie) was born, I came out crying. It was December 10, 1945. I didn't need a smack on my ass, but the doctors gave me one anyway. They said, "Shut up." It didn't work; I've been talking ever since.

My twin brother Jackie and I were born at Rockaway Beach, Queens, New York. The hospital was near the Atlantic Ocean off the beach; I guess that is why we always liked the water and sand. We were only three pounds each, so we stayed a little longer than most other babies in the hospital did and until we were five pounds. I guess we were good, because after a few weeks our parents took us home.

We grew up in Howard Beach, an area that was quiet except for the buses, trains and planes that went around our house all day and night. It was a nice place in Queens, New York, about fifteen miles from Manhattan. There was some farmland still around, and we played in the fields almost every day. We always got in trouble. Mary's farm, a few blocks from our own house, was always a fun place where we could hide in the old barn and hang out as long as farmer Joe didn't see us. We threw rocks near the cows when the farmers were milking them and then ran away, the cows would run too. The farmer knew who we were and he would tell our parents and the punishment would follow.

Jerry Byrne

There was always something bad that one of us did even as babies that got us in trouble. When we were around two years old, there were many milk strikes by the unions in the New York area and my father had to travel to New Jersey to get us milk. One day my mother had a few cartons of milk at the bottom of the carriage we were in and went inside the house with two other packages. When she came out, Jackie and I had punched holes in the cardboard milk containers with twigs we got from a nearby tree. My father wanted to kill us. We were brats. We were also loveable and cute, the twins, the prize, but my father still wanted to kill us.

We were out-of-control angels with our own language, that's what our neighbors said about us. My brother, Dennis, was the only one who knew what we were talking about. He would translate what we said to my mother. Today, we know that twins, creating their own language is not unusual, but at the time, my parents thought there was something wrong with us. I wish we had a tape recorder at that time, but no one in the family could afford one.

There weren't many places we couldn't go within 5 to 8 miles from our house. We were kids, so we did go to places that we were told not to. Many times we walked on the tracks that were for the Long Island Rail Road, in back of our house. It was a shortcut to other locations that are now part of the eighth-avenue subway line. We also played in and around Idlewild Airport. Name was changed December 1963 to The John F. Kennedy International Airport. It was a short distance from the back of our house, around two miles, and was a fun place to play. We walked to the

International Building in the middle of the airport on Saturdays, where there were many items from other countries that we could buy for a few dollars and spend hours in the stores looking around. As long as our mother did not catch us, everything was ok. We had all of Jamaica Bay, the Rockaways and Howard Beach to do whatever we wanted also to go where we wanted, and go we did.

Jackie and I went to Our Lady of Grace, R. C. School, two blocks from our house. The school was from the first to eighth grade. We were lucky to get out. In school, we would always get 100% on many of the tests that were taken—50% each.

We didn't like the nuns or studying.

Since we both had bad teeth a trip to the dentist was required many times every year. We usually made an appointment in the morning, so we would get out of going to class. The dentist was a few miles away and we had to take a bus to get there, which we never did and always walked to waste time. We used the bus money on candy. When we returned to the school, we would hide downstairs from the classroom or play outside until a few minutes before twelve o'clock. Then we would report back to the nuns that we were back and ready for school, just in time for lunch. We would run home laughing that we fooled the nuns again.

More than a few times, we were put in the closet in the back of the classroom, for being disruptive. When we told our mother about this, she came to the school to speak to the nuns. Sister Mary said, "Mrs. Byrne, we would never do that to these angels." My mother left smiling, while Jackie and I got put back in the closet for the rest of the afternoon. I didn't think we were that bad just because we changed our nametags and our seats many times, sometimes twice a day. We even changed our clothes. My mother said that she put tags on our cribs but wasn't sure if she put the right twin back in the correct crib. So it's quite possible that we were not who we thought we were.

I think that the nuns couldn't put up with us any longer, so after eight years in school, they graduated us. The sisters (the nuns) had a party when we left in June 1959. After graduation day, all the nuns in the school went on vacation for a few weeks, happy to be rid of the two angels who were always in trouble. We were thirteen years old and happy to get out of this school.

One day, a friend of my brother David came over to our house and started to push us around. I guess we were ten years old at the time. This was not the first time he pushed us around and took candy from us. He was a wiseass and also around three hundred pounds. He liked to eat, so we made donuts for him, after my brother and the fat ass took a walk to the store down the block. They consisted of colored clay and baby power. I held a small box with the donuts in it under my arm, as they returned from the store and walked through the front door. Fat ass said, "What do you have there?"

"Nothing for you," I said. He grabbed the box and stuffed one donut in his mouth. He was happy until he bit down, into the clay and it went between his teeth. Jackie and I ran out of the house and jumped over the fence in the back yard before David's friend could kill us.

David was laughing and said to his friend, "Leave the kids alone." We never forgot that and I don't think his friend did either. "Don't fuck with the Byrne brothers."

We got our first job during the summer of 1959, a few days after graduation day, renting beach umbrellas and chairs in Rockaway Beach, on 116th street. I remembered the owners, two old Jewish men that wanted us to work our ass off for fifty cents an hour, plus tips. They would tell us every day that for forty years they had been renting the umbrellas and chairs (the same ones). They knew what the people at the beach wanted. Day after day, they told us how much they knew about selling and business. If one chair or umbrella were stolen, these two old men would cry for days. We worked from eight in the morning until six at night, seven days a week. We were happy to get a job that was outside and on the beach.

Every week after getting paid, we always got a half a gallon of ice cream each and some type of cake from the Atlantic and Pacific supermarket. Since both of us liked to read, we would spend the rest of our money on books, comic books, that is.

In September 1959, we started high school, about eight miles from our house. We couldn't go to the school that was only two miles away because of my other two brothers. They were kicked out and had a lot of problems with their teachers. Both of them were always starting fights with other students and the teachers and skipping class. My mother didn't want her angels to get in trouble at John Adams High School, so off we went to Thomas Edison High in Jamaica, Queens. We had to take three buses to get there. After the first week, we stopped taking the third bus. It was only a mile to the school, from the third bus stop, and because of all the stops it made would take twenty minutes to get us there. We didn't want to wait for the bus and started to run to the school. After school, we would race down the hill, with a few others guys usually to catch an early train at the station. If we missed that train, we would have to wait thirty minutes for the next one. We would only have to get one bus after the train ride to get home. Kids today don't even want to walk three or four blocks to get to school. Being lazy was not in our blood. We did join the track team, but the black students would always outrun us. After a few months, we stopped going.

High school was good for us; we were always active in sports. Running, Boxing, Karate, Judo, Swimming, and Handball were a few of the things that we both enjoyed. We joined the gymnastic team, which pushed us to our limit; we tried to be the best.

We also got help from our Uncle Nick, in his basement once a week with his friend Jonesy on the art of boxing and wrestling. That went on for years; while we were in high school and gave us many memories of learning the many moves and fighting stands from my Uncle. Jackie and I kept them in shape, as we were being taught by them. I always remembered that Jonesy never liked to box. Jackie and I were faster and would hit him many times. We never liked to wrestle with him because he was good. Once he got you in a hold, you were finished. Uncle Nick beat us in everything. It was our goal to beat him, but that never happened. After an hour or two, we would go home worn out, while Nick and Jonesy would go upstairs and have a beer and some snacks. We looked forward to going across the street every week to see if we could beat them. The rule was that we had to box and wrestle with each of them, and we did.

While in school we got along with most of the kids in our classes. No one was ever going to pick on us because we always watched each other's backs. If we got into any fights, it is not that the other brother would jump in, but we would make sure that it was a fair fight.

One day after we ran to the bottom of the hill, we stopped in a department store a block away from the train station to buy something.

Some guy came up to Jackie and said, "Give me a fucking dime or I will kill you." I was standing next to this guy and asked him to repeat what he just said. "Just give me a fucking dime kid," he said. Jackie punched him twice in the mouth and then pushed him into a rack of suits, the coats and pants that were neatly hanging on the racks went all over the floor. When the cops came, the guy said he asked for the time and this wiseass kid, (pointing at Jackie) started to punch him. He said he was on parole and didn't want to cause any trouble. The cops told us to go home and locked up the guy that got punched.

Some people say that twins can read each other's minds. Well we almost could. I knew that Jackie was going to punch this guy. At times, we could sense what the other was going to do and the next moves were recorded in our minds. We knew the moves that each of us would use and where he would be standing during a fight. We practiced kicking and punching to our rear as fast as we could many times. Each of us had to know where the other brother would be, so neither one got kicked accidentally in the balls. We were there to protect each other. From elementary school to Vietnam, we always had each other's backs.

One day on our train ride home, a guy sat next to us and said he had a knife; in his pocket and wanted some money. I said, "No, but if you take your hand out of your pocket, we will kill you before you can stand up." The guy said he was just kidding. He didn't expect two teenagers to stand up to him.

One day when I was walking down the street near the beach in Rockaway, I heard Jackie call me. I turned around, but didn't see anyone. I heard him again and he said, "I will see you in a few minutes." I didn't see anyone on the street and continued to walk towards our house a few blocks away. When I turned the next corner, Jackie was walking toward me. He said he was just thinking of me because he wanted to play handball, and he sensed I was near. We didn't think it was strange because we had always done that. I wish that feeling could be with me again. Maybe someday when I feel his presents around me he will be there.

In the gym at school, they had a speed bag and a heavy bag, which we were good at punching. My father always had a heavy bag and speed bag in the garage that he taught us how to hit. The garage was in the back of the house until my father, with the help of my Uncle Nick, built an extension to the house by adding an extra bedroom. In 1960, both bags were put in the basement. We punched at the bags, almost every day for an hour, hitting them as fast and hard as we could. I think that when the other kids saw us working out, in the school gym, they had second thoughts about causing any trouble with us. We did not look for trouble, but also we didn't want anyone else to give us any. We wanted to be always ready to fight if we had to.

One morning, an hour before we were going to catch our bus to school, my oldest brother David said he would drive us. We were happy about that; it was a cold morning, and to sit in a warm car instead of a cold bus put smiles on our faces. David was having a cup of coffee a few minutes before we were to leave, when there was a knock on the door.

My mother asked, "Who is it?" The answer came quickly, the police. With those words, David's coffee cup fell on the floor. He ran as fast as he could toward the back door, opened it, and was surprised to see police officers standing there with two guns pointing at him.

They said, "Good morning David. You are going for a ride in our car."

David had to serve three months in a New York City prison, time for five thousand dollars of unpaid parking tickets that had been ripped up, sometimes in front of the officer who gave it to him, over the last ten years. David also got his driving license taken away in New York and most of the surrounding states. He lucked out because a fire in the motor vehicle's office in New Jersey had destroyed all the records. He got the license back a few months after the fire. We always thought he started the fire.

Jackie and I had to run our ass off, to catch a bus for school. We were late that day, one of only a few times in four years. David did many things that could have gotten him killed or thrown in jail each day. He was a con artist who never wanted to pay for anything. Many times when he didn't pay, he got someone else to put out the money. One day he went to a car dealer in Queens, New York, for a new 1959 Lincoln. He didn't have to put any money down, and in a couple of hours, after signing many papers, that he would pay back the loan, the new car was parked in the front of my parents' home. David sitting at the kitchen table was telling Jackie and me that this is the only way to drive, pointing to the new car. "So get yourselves a new car," he said as he started to laugh. He never paid, any of the monthly charges. Ten months later, the dealer did repossess the car. They told David by letter, a few days after they took the car, that they were pressing charges against him. That night, he broke into the dealer's lot and got the Lincoln back. He called the dealer and told them to drop all charges, or they would never see him or the car again. They did drop the charges. David drove to Florida the next day and called the dealer to pick up their car in South Beach. He had balls.

Another time David went upstate for a job to get out of Manhattan. He went to a construction site and told the foreman on that job that Joe from the city told him to come up and run this job. The foreman said, "Fuck you, this is my job.

David looked at him and said, "Why don't you tell that to fucking Joe." I am sure he would love to hear from you." No one fucked with Joe from the city.

The foreman, after thinking about what may happen to his family or himself said, "Fuck it, the job is yours."

The next morning, David called four of his friends up to the job site and they were all put on the payroll. They sat in a bar with a couple of girls on their laps across the street from the job every day for the next 6 weeks. This was a big party for them. The owner of the building came to the job and realized that there was no work being done, and called Joe.

"What's with this worker named David that you sent up here? Are you trying to fuck me?"

Joe said, "David who?" David heard about the phone call from one of the clerks in the office and took off for California that morning. He knew that his body would be buried in the woods if they got him. He stayed out there hiding for five years. He had balls.

For the most part, our four years in high school was enjoyable. We did like going to this school. It was a Vocational School; we both studied printing and took up space.

Our first job was good, but the second job the following summer was better. For the next three years, during the summer months, we worked on the beach, selling ice cream for four or five hours a day. We had to carry a box of ice cream and juice that weighted thirty-five pounds—while walking in the sand. We made money every day, around ten or fifteen dollars plus tips. This was better than working for minimum wage, which was only one dollar an hour. We knew most of the people sitting on the beach and boardwalk, maybe not all by name, but by face. The police also would help us out at times, if we needed them.

They always got free food and beer from the stores at the beach, so they looked out for us. There were people, selling juice or ice cream without a license in the area where Jackie and I worked. Jackie walked over to one guy—(usually they were older than us and in their twenties: we were sixteen years old at that time) and told him to leave the beach. "Fuck you, kid," the guy said, "you leave the area or I will kick your ass." Jackie punched him a few times in the head, and kicked him in the balls. The guy got up and ran to the boardwalk for help from one of his friends. Seeing what was going on, I waved to a cop that we knew that was sitting on the boardwalk, having a beer. This cop would help anyone who worked on the storefronts from 108th to 126th street. The cop waved me toward him. He asked me what the problem was. In a few minutes, the guy Jackie hit and his friend were in the Paddy wagon, going to jail. (Paddy Wagon is an English term, used for the wagon that was used, to pick up drunken Irishmen, after a fight. The English did not give a shit if that was a correct term or not.) During our many years in Rockaway Beach, we saw the Paddy wagon full every Friday and Saturday night. Most of the time they were Irishmen, who had one drink too many.

All this walking did keep us in shape. After selling ice cream and drinks and walking for hours on the beach, we would play handball for a few hours. After dinner, the boxing gloves came on for an hour.

Jackie and I would run along the beach, a couple of miles each morning before we started work. There were not many people who could keep up with us. After listening to my brother David for years, we were ready for the Marines. Were the Marines ready for us? In our minds, we were the best. Could we keep up with the best? Would our dreams be happy or sad? Only time would tell.

Jackie and I were brainwashed, at an early age by my brother David, who went in the Marine Corps in 1955 and served for three years. David told us many times each day that we could never be Marines. We were not tough enough, strong enough, or good enough to be in the military. Growing up we always wanted to be like David, a tough Marine. Both of us, decided to go and enlist. Since the recruiting office was a short distance from our school, Thomas Edison, we waited until after we got out of school at three in the afternoon to go talk to the recruiting sergeant. We wanted to know what it would take for us to be Marines. We were told to take a test and have our parents sign a form giving the Marines the right to have us join their ranks because we were underage. Signing the papers didn't come easy for my mother, but my father said, "OK." My mother eventually signed the papers, because there were no wars going on in 1963.

The next day, we returned to the recruiting Sergeant. He was smiling and happy that we got our parents to sign the letter. He told us we would be known as Marines forever after boot camp. He told us that the Marine Corps was happy to have us in their ranks and we would be called Marines. Only a handful of recruits could past the test. He handed us the papers and said, "Sign them and be Marines. The best of the best sign the papers and become Marines." Jackie and I were on top of the world; our smiling faces could be seen from a distance. The papers were signed, and the day was September 18, 1963, three months after we graduated. When we told David that we were going to be Marines, he started to laugh and laughed every time he looked at us.

Shaking his head, while he looked at us, he said, "Fucking stupid pieces of shit." We didn't know why David said that, but someday we did find out. We would soon be in for the surprise of a lifetime. There was nothing that could prepare us for what was coming. The memory of that first day in Boot Camp would always be in our minds.

CHAPTER 2

THE PLEDGE: THE MORNING NOT TO BE FORGOTTEN

The sun was shining into the window, behind my house, a bright yellow happy face to start our day. My father was sitting at the table eating bacon and eggs. After his fifth cup of coffee, he was almost finished eating when he said, "It is going to be a long day for you guys." That would be my twin brother Jackie and I. We were up early and had already eaten and packed our suitcases. We were packing our suitcases like we were going on a vacation to Disneyland. We didn't know at the time, but everything that we had with us would be sent back home when we got to Parris Island. After a stack of pancakes and eggs, we were ready for anything. Or so we thought. We couldn't wait to go on this trip. My father was going to drive us to New York City, Whitehall Street. This day finally came, September 18, 1963. We would be sworn in as United States Marines at Whitehall Street in a few hours. We were seventeen years old and ready to take on the world. We gave our mother a big hug and kiss. She was crying because her angels were leaving her.

After an hour or two of driving from Queens, we arrived in front of a tall building on Whitehall Street. We said our goodbyes to our father. No hugs or kisses, but he looked like he was sad to see us go. Men of that era didn't show emotions towards others, a handshake is usually all we got.

He said he would be down for our graduation from Parris Island, Marine Corps Boot Camp, South Carolina, in a few months.

Everyone was nice to us, and waved to us as we entered the building. We had soda, cake, and smiles on our faces while we waited to be sworn in. We didn't know it at this time but we were lambs going to be fed to the lions. We couldn't wait. Jackie and I were going to be Marines. The hour was upon us. Jackie and I raised our right hand and pledged our lives to this great country, and to the Marine Corps. Never turn your back on either one.

As we were leaving the room after being sworn in, standing tall and proud, talking and laughing with the other new Marines, our eyes spotted someone we knew. Jackie called out to the sergeant that we talked to at the recruiting office. He was our friend. He had talked to us like we were brothers before today. "Sergeant Jones!" Jackie yelled, "We are here, we are Marines now."

I said, "What's happening man?" How are you doing? We are on the same team now, like one family, brothers together and forever.

The sergeant looked at us with hate in his eyes, ran as fast as he could at Jackie, grabbed him around the throat, and pushed him into the nearest wall.

Sergeant Jones was yelling, screaming, "Who the fuck do you think you are. Who are you talking to, maggot? You are a piece of shit and you will always be a piece of shit. You will only call me Sir, is that clear you piece of shit, or I will kill you before you even get on that bus!" He looked over at me; his eyes seem to be on fire. He ran over to me, grabbed me around the face, and said, "Do you understand that maggot? Don't you ever look at me again, or I will rip your eyes out. Is that clear maggot?" I started to shake.

I said, "Yes Sir!" as loud as I could. So much for all of us always being lifetime brothers.

We both started to sweat and shake at this potential violent act toward us. We thought this sergeant was our friend? We would soon be in for the surprise of a lifetime.

For the rest of our time at Whitehall Street, we sat in a chair with our backs against the wall. There were other Marines walking by but we wouldn't look at them. After an hour or two, we were told to get on the bus. They didn't ask us to get on the bus, they screamed, "Get on the fucking bus now, move it, move it, do it now people; we don't have all day, do it now!"

Jackie and I ran to the bus, we were the first ones on and got seats in the back next to a window. We watched the people of the city walking fast on the sidewalk next to the bus, going to work in these tall office buildings. It would be a few years before we enjoyed those sights again.

It was a long ride to Parris Island, South Carolina, around fifteen hours or more and the bus stopped three or four times, so we could all use the rest rooms and stretch our legs. On the last few hours of the ride, most of us fell asleep. We didn't wake up until someone woke us.

"Get off; get off, get off, you fucking maggots! Now, Now, Now, this is not your mommies' lap you are on. This is my fucking bus. Get off, get off, get off. Do it now!" With those words, this crazy guy was grabbing anyone within his reach, and throwing them off the bus. Some of the guys were pushed so hard that they landed on the ground. One guy broke his arm.

Some crazy fuck was yelling for us to get at attention, up off the ground, stand up. "Do you maggots think that you are going to sleep all fucking day? This is my Marine Corps and you maggots are fucking it up!" We didn't know what getting to attention meant. But we found out soon enough. We found out when this guy, with a strange looking hat, stood in front of Jackie screaming, "What are you looking at you piece of shit? Do you like me; do you want to fuck me? Get your eyes off me and stand tall, don't fucking move." This scared the hell out of us. These are our drill instructors. Three of the meanest looking men we had ever seen. One of the drill instructors kicked a guy so hard he fell to the ground. He was standing over him yelling, "Why don't you cry you piece of shit. You fucking maggot. "Start crying for your mommy's tits, you won't be sucking on them anymore. This is my Marine Corps and you will do as I say. You fucking maggots are mine now."

It took the recruit a few minutes to get up off the ground and he had tears in his eyes. He also had to go to the hospital.

There was nothing that could prepare us for what was coming. The memories of that day would always be on our mind.

Did we sign up to be with a group of mentally unbalanced people? Are we going to be like them? I hope not.

CHAPTER 3

THE DAY THE WORLD STOPPED

There were sixty of us.

The first few days we all thought we were in another world. We were in the Marine Corps world, where the Gods (the drill instructors) always had the last word and they were always right. We didn't want their eyes on us. We got our heads shaved and were issued new clothes. Clothes and haircuts were the same for everyone. Sit down, shut up, and get your head shaved. There were no choices. We got two pairs of shoes, a pair of black dress shoes, a pair of brown dress shoes, and also black combat boots. There were no sandals or sneakers worn by the recruits. We may be in the south, but there were no sandy beaches for us. By the time we left boot camp, we could see our reflection on the tips of our shoes and boots, which we had to shine every day. Even when there was a shine on them, the drill instructor may come over to you and step on the boot, or pick it up and drop it in the muddy water out back and tell you to do it again. The clothes given to us were socks, shirts, trousers, underwear, overcoat and a jacket, which were for everyday use. The uniforms came later. I didn't know until months later that we had to pay for our clothes with our first paycheck of ninety dollars. At least they were paying us ninety dollars a month. We had to run everywhere and we all ran to the medical center the next morning. The doctors were lined up with their needles and we were given every vaccine that you could think of. There is something wrong with running to a doctor to get a shot when you're not sick. Being a wise ass, my brother Jackie made the mistake of asking one of the doctors if he liked the way his ass looked when he was getting a shot. That did not get over too well; Jackie got a few extra shots from the doctor in his ass, and a punch in the face. He couldn't sit down for hours, or eat anything the rest of the day. We ran everywhere, no one walked. Run to the mess hall, walk fast on the line for food, and pick up one knife, one fork, and one spoon. Don't stop to talk to anyone and don't ask for more food. Eat everything that is put on your plate. How do the drill instructors keep track of all the new recruits? Eyes are on us all day, seven days a week and twenty-four hours a day. Obey every command or get the shit knocked out of you.

Two or three times a day, we would get a head call, which is another name for the bathroom. We were told to take a shit and you do it, even when there are twenty guys looking at you and waiting their turn. There are about ten toilet bowls next to each other and the drill instructor gives you two minutes to go. Sometimes he would stand there with a fucking stopwatch and say, go. If you think you will take more time, it is not going to happen in boot camp. The drill instructors will grab you and throw you on the floor as you are going, not a pleasant sight. All hell will break out if your shit hits the floor instead of the bowl. The three words starting with the letter "s" in boot camp are shit, shower, and shave. You may get five minutes for all three, but not often. Time to relax is one thing that the recruit doesn't have.

Every day we would scream as we were running, "Here we go, every day, up the hill, down the hill, through the hill, Marine Corps, all the way." Marines getting brain washed, maybe. Jackie and I were hiding in the middle of the platoon, after what happened in New York City on Whitehall Street and on the bus, when it arrived in Parris Island, we didn't want to stand out. We were lucky for the first two weeks. Then we got mail from home.

This should have been a happy occasion but not for Jackie or myself.

We had our dinner in the mess hall and ran back to the barracks. We were told we had mail from home. Everyone was happy. All lined up at attention in front of our bunks, the drill instructor called out a name, it sounded like Byrne but I wasn't sure. He called it again, much louder this time and then screamed so loud, that no one wanted to move. "Get the fuck up here," he said. From all corners of the room you could hear, "Here Sir, here Sir, here Sir." The three of us all ran as fast as we could. We stood at attention in front of the man who was now God and had the first letter from our parents in his hands. Standing tall and happy to be called, Jackie and I and someone else that had a name that sounded like Byrne, stood in front of the drill instructor. The drill instructor looked at us in disbelief.

"Three people, three useless pieces of shit. Maggots, with the same name, this can't be. Can't be," he said. "This is not real." What is your name he screamed at each of us? With that we screamed back one at a time, "Byrne Sir," "Byrne Sir," and "Burnt Sir."

He looked at Burnt and said, "Is your name Byrne?"

Burnt said, "No Sir. I thought you called my name Sir."

The drill instructor screamed "You! Do I look like a fucking female sheep to you? Do you think that you can fuck me? Do you fuck sheep? Is that what you farm boys like to do? Is that what you want to do? Do you want a piece of my ass Maggot?"

Burnt screamed, "No Sir."

The drill instructor screamed, "Why are you standing up here you piece of shit?" He then punched him twice in the face. "Get back to your spot in front of your bunk at attention, before I kill you. Move it, move it, move it!"

Tears in his eyes, he ran back in front of his bunk, blood on the side of his face, a tooth loose, shaking and hoping that the drill instructor never calls his name again. He would like to get a letter from home, but after this, he prayed all night that his parents lost his address. He didn't want to die.

"Now there were two. My eyes must be playing tricks on me," the drill instructor said, as he eyed my brother Jackie and I. We were standing tall and looking straight ahead in front of the drill instructor. The drill instructor screamed at me again, asking, "What is your name?"

"Byrne Sir," I said with a smile. With that, I got punched hard in the gut for smiling and he pushed me to the floor.

23

He looked at my brother Jack and said, "What's your name, Maggot?"

"Byrne Sir," he said, but he didn't smile. He got punched hard in the face anyway for looking like me. The drill instructor than kick him in the balls and pushed him to the floor.

"Get up and stand tall, you pieces of shit," yelled the drill instructor. Jackie and I jumped up as fast as we could. Thinking that the drill instructor would be impressed on how fast we were able to get up after being hit. We found out later that the drill instructors never show anyone how impressed they were with the actions of any recruit.

The drill instructor let out a loud scream and said, "Why me? Why did fucking God do this to me? Why God, why are there two lowlife, useless scrum bags in my house? Two maggots dumb and dumber, useless pieces of shit, standing in front of me that looked and acted the same way. Why me God?" he said again and again. He turned and left the room shaking his head like a crazy man, sweat dripping down the side of his face and waving his hands, from side to side. The drill instructor was screaming and hitting himself in the head many times yelling "Why God, why?" We didn't move. We didn't look at or talk to each other. Standing there at attention, eyes straight ahead, thinking that this is the end of our time in the Marine Corps. Is the drill instructor going to come back to kill us?

What did we do that was so bad that we made someone run out of the squad bay? We did not know and we did not move but we would soon find out.

After a few minutes, the drill instructor came back. He had three other drill instructors' from the other platoons with him. Our drill instructor was screaming and looking at us. "Look what God did to me," he yelled to the other drill instructors. Each drill instructor came over in front of us and we did not move. One of the Sergeants hit me in the stomach, turns to Jackie and asks, "Did you feel that?"

"No Sir," he said, and with that remark, he got hit as hard as the drill instructor could hit him.

He said, "You feel that now, you piece of shit?"

"Why did God fuck my friend Sergeant Jones? Tell me what he did wrong. Are you friends with God?" he asked. We did not know at that time that there is no right or wrong answer to that question. I said, "Yes Sir," and I was then hit hard in the face and was told to tell my friend God to leave his friend, Sergeant Jones alone.

"Do you know why God did this to us?" the other drill instructor asked. "No Sir," I said and got hit again for not knowing what my friend God had against Sergeant Jones. This went on for the next ten minutes, Sergeant Jones was yelling "Why me God, why me? " I go to church, I pray, I gave money last week, so why are you doing this to me?" He was screaming, walking around in circles, why, why, why? We had to get on our knees and pray to God for fifteen minutes and repeat over and over to leave Sergeant Jones alone.

"God must be evil to do this to Sergeant Jones," the other drill instructors said. Without our letters from home, we were told to go back to our position in front of our bunk. We were not allowed to look at anyone in the room. Our faces had to be toward the bunk bed. We had to say over and over, "Forgive Sergeant Jones, God." That lasted for only a few minutes. It seemed like forever.

This type of action in boot camp is normal for the drill instructors to do. We were shaking and confused. This is what the instructors wanted.

There are no clocks in boot camp. This was the beginning of our time in hell.

The other recruits didn't look at any of the drill instructors as they entered, or left the room. They didn't want to be in the spotlight and have the same thing happening to them. Their eyes were not blinking, or moving, or they too would be punched to the ground by the drill instructors, if they saw any looks from them in their direction.

The other drill instructors left the room laughing and yelling, loud enough for us to hear, "Why does God hate you so much? This is a nightmare for you, Sergeant Jones." Garbage in your platoon, I hope you can handle these two fucking maggots!"

The drill instructor knew that tomorrow would be another day to break our balls and told us and the rest of the platoon to go to sleep and pray that God will forgive Sergeant Jones.

The next day Jackie and I stood in front of the Captain of our company. They didn't want any parents calling their congressman about their kids not getting any mail. The Captain was informed by the drill instructor that there were two maggots that looked alike in his platoon.

The Captain came over to us and gave us our letters from home. The Captain told us that if the drill instructors hit or abused us in any way, report to him immediately. Both Jackie and I were happy that the Captain said that. At least the Captain will be looking out for us. Maybe we won't be punched or kicked any more. Our minds soon were fearful of the drill instructors once again when we saw that the Captain and the senior drill Instructor, laughing and pointing at us. The Captain with one hand did an upper cut punch with his fist and with the other hand, had two fingers up, and pointing at us. We knew now that we were in trouble and the captain lied to us. If we reported anything to him, we would probably die. We had to watch each other's backs, but how do we do that at 17 years old against the Sons of God? Boot camp was not going to be easy for us. Physically we could do anything but it was the mental attitude we had trouble dealing with. We didn't think that being twins were going to be a problem with the drill instructors but it was.

It did not take long before every drill instructor in Parris Island knew that there were two shit birds in Sergeant Jones' platoon. Two fucking lookalike shit birds, in the same platoon. More drill instructors came over to us one at a time, and stood in front of us. Each one would punch one of us, and ask the same question to the other one, "Did that hurt you, maggot?" If we said, "Yes Sir," we would get hit harder for not being a hard ass Marine. If we said, "No Sir," we would get hit even more for being a pussy. With the drill instructors, the recruit never wins. We thought that the days before this day was our time in hell, we were wrong, it was just beginning. It seemed to us that everyone was having a great time abusing us. Laughing and hitting us all day. We looked at each other when we could and said to each other "Did we really volunteer for this?"

We wanted to run out of the main gate and go home. That was not going to happen. We were told the first day that the alligator's in the water around the base liked to eat, new, fresh recruits. We decided to stick it out for now. The alligators will have to stay hungry, unless some other recruit fucks up.

CHAPTER 4

THE SWIM

It was five o'clock in the morning and the sun wasn't up yet, but platoon 272 had to wake up. "Get up, get up, get up. You girls are in for some fun today," said the Marine drill instructor as he grabbed anyone within his reach that didn't get out of bed on his command and pulled them to the floor. Any recruit who wasn't quick enough got kicked until they stood at attention in front of their bunk. "We are going swimming today girls. This is a fun day." The senior drill instructor as he walked by me, looked me in the eye and said, "Can you swim, maggot?"

I said, "Yes Sir." With that, he hit my brother Jackie who was standing in front of his bunk next to me. I forgot to say "Yes Sir, Sir."

"When I put your face under the water we will see how long you can hold your breath maggot," said the drill instructor.

"Yes Sir, Sir," I replied. We thought someone would die today. I hoped it would not be one of us. The first few weeks and every week after the first mail call were not happy weeks for Jackie or me. Every time that we were marching, or running and not in step with the drill instructors command of left, – right, – left one of us got punched. We kept telling ourselves that it will get better tomorrow, but it didn't.

"Left, right, left, who do we love, Marine Corps!" This screaming goes on for hours. No wonder marines get brainwashed before getting out of boot camp.

Together, Jackie and I were unbeatable in the water. We grew up on the beach, in Rockaway, New York, but we were not going to tell this scumbag that we could swim at least a mile with no problems. In rockaway beach, we liked to ride the waves into the sand. The bigger the waves were, the better they were to ride. We even had a policeman tell us one hot summer day, to get out of the water because of a storm and heavy rain coming into the area. We said no, fuck you. The cop told the lifeguard not to go into the water after us.

"If they get into any trouble, let them drown," he said. We didn't care; we were too young to die. We would also challenge each other to see who could stay under the water the longest. Some days he won, other days, I won. We were twins, and we loved the water. It was a game for us.

After running two miles, we went to the mess hall to eat. A few guys couldn't eat because they were thinking about the water and the fact that they couldn't swim. If not for the drill instructors, it would have been every enjoyable to be in a large swimming pool. While we ran back to our barracks, Jackie and I were thinking that we would be putting on a bathing suit and enjoying a nice swim. We were wrong.

The drill instructors were screaming at us to put on all our 782 gear, which consisted of a field pack, a pack filled with extra clothes, canteens, a small metal plate (to eat out of) and one knife, fork and spoon and of course we had to put on our boots. Altogether, we had about forty pounds of extra weight on our backs. We were only maggots and cow shit at this time. We weren't allowed to go to the rifle range yet (that would come in a few weeks). The weight of the rifle would add an extra ten pounds to our equipment. The rifles were still locked in a rifle rack, because we weren't Marines yet.

Everything is timed, so that you only get a few minutes to be ready.

"Put everything on and get outside! Now! Now! Now!" Platoon 272, was ready to work up a sweat. The pool was a mile or two away and we didn't walk. The drill instructors were the only ones that had bathing suits and sneakers on. Yelling the whole way to run faster and keep in step.

Thank God, Jackie and I were forgotten about for now. Many of the guys in the platoon couldn't swim and some of them were shaking with fear. Some of them had never been in a pool or seen a beach. We were concerned about some of the guys but also happy that the drill instructors eyes were not on us. A handful of the guys had weight problems. Some of them were thirty or forty pounds overweight. They didn't have to go to the motivation platoon yet. That platoon had one purpose. The drill instructors gave everyone in that platoon hell all day long for 24 hours a day until those recruits could keep up with the other recruits. Many of the recruits would pass out from physical exertion or the beatings. They had to either gain or lose weight, and they had to exercise constantly. It was worse than boot camp. It was not uncommon for some recruits to attempt suicide. I don't know how some of these guys ran to the pool area. It was probably due to a fear that the drill instructors would kill them in the water if they didn't make it running and had to walk to the pool.

There were only two guys that passed out and had to be taken to the hospital. They couldn't swim and had to be forced off the high driving board, to get them into the water. When they did hit the water, they couldn't get back up to the surface. They were overweight and had an extra forty pounds of weight on their backs. We thought that the drill instructors were going to kill them.

I was next on the diving board to jump in. My brother Jackie was already in the water. He did the right thing, jumped in and got out as soon as possible after swimming to the other side of the pool. In my mind, I kept saying don't do anything stupid. I was in the clear, forgotten about by the drill instructors all day. But I wanted to show off in the water. Just one of many mistakes that I made in boot camp, but this was on the top of the list for being the stupidest. When I jumped off the high diving board, I went straight to the bottom and stayed there. After a minute under the water, I stretched out my hands and leg and made believe I was dead, while staying at the bottom of the pool. Everyone around the pool went into a panic. The lifeguards, emergency personnel, and of course the drill instructors were all screaming for someone to get in the water and get that maggot out. Five or six people jumped in to save me from drowning, thinking that I was dead, or soon would be.

Three of the lifeguards grabbed me from the bottom of the pool and took me to the top of the water. They were all out of breath and in a panic.

I thought it was comical that I did this. I held my breath until I was cleared of the water. I could have held my breath for another thirty seconds. When I got to the surface, I started to laugh. The drill instructors didn't think that was funny. If someone dies on their watch, all hell would break loose. Only a few years before I got to Parris Island, six marines died while the drill instructors were pushing them into the water at night around Parris Island. They were forced to run in the water up to their necks and all of them drowned. This was known as the Ribbon Creek Incident, April 8, 1956.

I think that I was the first marine to be water boarded by friendly personnel. This was in 1963. The drill instructors all took turns holding me under the water. "We should kill this Maggot, and give his worthless body to the gators," the senior drill instructor said. After many minutes of torture, by holding my face in the water, they let me go back to the platoon. I guess I was lucky, that they didn't kill me or take it out on my brother Jack, who was trying not to laugh and not get caught smiling.

Maybe someday, the drill instructors would laugh about it, but I don't think it would be anytime soon. They definitely didn't laugh today.

I was told to run as fast as I could back to the barrack. I was soaking wet. I was hoping that was enough punishment for one day and I could now rest up. A few minutes after I got to the barrack the rest of the platoon ran in. They were told to clean up and get ready for bed. There were other things that had to be done before I said, "Good night, Sir." I had to do a few hundred jumping jacks, with my wet clothes on and all my field equipment in a wet pack that was still on my back. Screaming the whole time, "I am an Idiot!" I guess I showed them that I could swim. My legs felt like they would fall off, but I couldn't show the pain. An hour passed and I was then told to clean up.

After I took a hot shower and cleaned all my equipment, I was told to get some sleep.

"Good night Sir."

"Good Night Maggot."

"Yes Sir; Sir."

For the next few days, I tried to hide in the background as much as possible. I tried to do everything right. I felt safe for now. Until the next time the drill instructor's eyes met mine.

CHAPTER 5

THE RIFLE RANGE

Three weeks in hell, which is the time we will spend on the rifle range doing what Marines do best. Some will fail to qualify. Two or three percent will fail to qualify in many platoons. One is too many for Platoon # 272.

The drill instructor came over to each of us and handed us our weapon. "This is your rifle; no one else's but yours. If you drop it or abuse it, take out your bayonet and kill yourself." The drill instructor said that many times. The second biggest sin in the Marine Corps is calling your rifle a gun. The first biggest sin is going UNQ (unqualified) on the rifle range with the rifle that the Marine Corps had given to you. You will treat your rifle like you would treat a woman, rub it and hold it every day. Be good to it and it will be good to you. Most of us in the platoon didn't even want the rifle at this time for fear that we would drop it and have to kill ourselves. In boot camp, our minds didn't belong to us. Recruits will be responsible for their rifle and know every part of it before he gets to fire it. After many hours of hearing about the rifle now, we finally got one.

"Shoot to kill, this is not a game. You Maggots will learn every part of the rifle, and quickly take it apart in the dark and put it back together again. If you scumbags screw up and embarrass me by failing and getting the "Maggie's Drawers' (a term used to indicate that the target was missed while shooting on the rifle range) when it is your turn to shoot, I will beat you into the ground and kick your ass out of my Marine Corps. Is that clear maggots? I want to hear you; you all better let me hear you, now."

"Yes Sir, Sir!"

"I can't hear you," he said again.

"Yes Sir! Sir" All sixty privates screamed, together, "Yes Sir!" as loud as they all could for the drill instructor to hear them. They were all praying that they could shoot a weapon to make the Marine Corps proud of them. Also that God will have mercy on their souls if they let down their drill instructor and have to kill themselves. Always remember that the drill instructors are the Sons of God.

Every morning John and I, along with everyone else, had to scream out in formation, "This is my rifle and this is my gun," (while grabbing your penis with one hand and your rifle with the other hand).

"One is for killing, the other for fun." If the drill instructors see you smiling while you say that, they will make you run around the base naked for hours, shooting and your rifle is not a joke in the Marine Corps.

The Marine instructors on the rifle range will teach almost everyone at Parris Island boot camp how to shoot a rifle. How well a recruit uses that knowledge is up to them. It is up to the drill instructor to teach every recruit how to kill with it, and kill you will.

The drill instructor was not finished with us yet. He walked in front of me and grabbed my rifle. It flew out of my hands with such force that I couldn't believe it. A Marine's rifle should not be taken away by anyone. With that, I got hit in the gut with the butt of the rifle. He gave it back to me with such force that I thought it would break my arms. Thank God I was able to hold on to my rifle and he moved on to someone else. We were all open for abuse that day, more today than other days. The drill instructors didn't want any failures today or any other day. My brother Jackie saw what happened and decided to hold on to his rifle at all cost. The drill instructors have been doing this for many years and they know all the tricks. He put his hands on Jackie's rifle softly and then kicked him in the balls as hard as he could.

"Have fun with that Maggot," he said. No matter how you think, you can't figure out the mind of the drill instructors, you are always wrong and they are always right. Being twins, Jack and I have to always be right at least half of the time. There were no broken jaws that day, but there was one arm almost broken and many bruises. The CID (Criminal Investigation Division) was not around that day. None of the recruits would have complained to them even if they were around, for fear of what could happen to them afterwards. The drill instructors always said, "If anyone wants to complain, do it. They always had a smile on their face when they were telling us this.

Jack and I never saw a rifle before boot camp. We played Cowboys and Indians while growing up. The Cowboys always won. Jack and I were always the Cowboys. We figured this would be an easy day. How hard could shooting be? Point and shoot. How hard can that be? Screw these drill instructors. We are the Byrne brothers. We can do it all. We were tough as long as the drill instructors were in another room and their eyes were not on us.

When you sit for hours with your rifle pressed into your shoulder and a sling wrapped around your arm your body becomes stiff. Your legs feel like they want to stretch out, but you are not allowed to move from that position, no matter how much it hurts. One Marine moved and was caught. The drill instructor grabbed the Marine around the neck and started to choke him. He didn't stop until the Marine passed out. We all thought he was dead. "That was what you get from moving without permission," screamed the "Son of God." After an hour, the Marine that we all thought had died started to move. I think we were all terrorized at that time. I endured the pain along with my brother Jackie and the other Marines from that day on. No one did any joking about anything on the rifle range.

The pain went on for days. Sitting, standing, and kneeling went on for hours at a time while we held the rifle in position to fire, being very careful not to drop the weapon no one wanted. Everyone put up with the pain because they didn't want the drill instructor near them. No one wanted to die over a stupid rifle, but never let the drill instructor read those thoughts in your mind. They will remain in my head forever. I prayed every day that the drill instructor couldn't read my mind and hoped to God that he never would.

The day finally came for us to shoot real bullets at a target with the rifle that the Marine Corps gave us. We better not let the Corps down.

If someone points their rifle at you, you shoot them before they shoot you. This is not a game. People die every day from bullets. Don't you be the one to die? "Is that clear Maggots?" he asked. "You all better listen to every word out of my mouth, is that clear Maggots?" he continued.

"Yes Sir, Sir!" we screamed as loud as we could.

Jackie and I, along with the rest of the platoon, received only three or four bullets on that first day. We never had a rifle in our hands before and that held true for many of the other men in the platoon. The drill instructors had to be careful at the rifle range because one of those bullets could be fired right at them. A rifle and bullets is a lot of power to be given to a 17 year old who had also been abused for the last few weeks. Every instructor on the range knows that. They also watch every move that the recruits make at all times. To not watch could mean a bullet in the head. Mentally, a recruit could snap at any time.

The bullets traveled out of the rifle toward their target when the trigger is pulled. Your fingers control the trigger and the trigger must be pulled softly and gently, like rubbing a "women's tit." The drill instructors told us that every day, and we had better learn to squeeze the trigger, softly every time. "Do it right, do you hear me? "Yes Sir, Sir!" is heard all day at the range.

We used the M1 rifle for a short time, known as the Garand, which had a weight of 9.5 pounds and fired a 7.62mm round, (.30 caliber) and had eight rounds to a magazine (a magazine is what holds the bullets in a case like container.) The Marine Corps replaced the M1 with the M14, around 1960. The M14 used a 20 round magazine, and was a better weapon. The Marine Corps used the M14 rifle in Vietnam until 1967 or 1968, and then it was replaced by the M16. The M16 rifle was a lighter weapon, 6.3 pounds (5.56 mm .223 calibers round) and had a 20 to 30 round magazine. In its infancy, the M16 would malfunction many times in combat and was probably the reason some Marines were killed. We used the M14 in booth camp, for close order drill and then for some of us to qualify with on the rifle range.

After many days of pain, being yelled at and getting hit by the drill instructors now we were ready, or hoped that we were ready, to qualify with the rifle that we didn't want. It took a few hours to complete the shooting from the 200 yards, 500 yards, and 1000 yards distance.

I was very nervous, just like everyone else. One shot at a time, praying to God that I didn't get a Maggie Drawers and would wind up dead by nightfall. I waited for a full minute after everyone else fired to fire my rifle. I wanted to do exactly what the drill instructor said. I was in shock when I saw that the first ten shots that I fired were dead center on the target. The drill instructors all came over to watch me. It scared the shit out of me. I didn't know what they were getting all excited with me about. I thought that everyone was getting bulls eyes. I was too scared to miss. Before firing a round, I would think about all the things the drill instructor said, even squeezing a woman's tit. Aim and squeeze the trigger, slowly for every round. I was getting the rounds in the center of the target repeatedly. I was happy with myself and then I fired and got the Maggie Drawers. My whole body started to shake. I thought the Sons of God were going to kill me where I sat. I got the Maggie Drawers. Shit! Now what will happen to me? I hope that the drill Instructor will let me talk to my brother Jack before I die. All of the drill Instructors around me said at the same time, "Take it easy, and squeeze that trigger, softly like a woman's tit. Take a deep breath and slowly squeeze the trigger."

The next shot, I did exactly what they said. I was at the 1000-yard line and pulled the trigger, as my eyes stayed on the center of the target. Sweat poured off me, while waiting for the outcome of my shot. It was only a couple of minutes, but it felt like an hour. The "Bull's Eye" flag was waved in front of the target. The drill instructors were jumping for joy? They were all patting each other on the back. I didn't know what they were so excited about. Never had I seen them like that before. I wanted to run as far away from the rifle range as I could and go home. Then the unexpected happened to me; the drill instructors all came over and told me that they were proud of me, "I made them proud," to be in their Marine Corps. Wow!

I shot, "EXPERT," on the rifle range with the rifle that I didn't even want. I was glad it was over. The tension for now was off my shoulders. I don't know how I did it, maybe because of the fear of failure, than sweat and pain, but I did it. I wouldn't be eaten by gators that night. It would be in my military records forever. They can't take that away from me. I was feeling good and proud of myself. For someone who never fired a weapon before, I felt good. I even had a smile on my face. But I turned around in the other direction so the drill instructors couldn't see me.

Good feelings don't last long in Boot Camp. My brother Jackie did not qualify with the rifle that he did not want. He received an "UNQ" (unqualified). I heard the drill instructor screaming at him, "You fucking pussy, you piece of shit." You are a disgrace to the Marine Corps. We should beat you into the ground Maggot for going UNQ." I looked to where Jackie was on the rifle range from the corner of my eyes. He was shaking and in tears. He didn't know what was going to happen to him. I didn't know what to do to help him. He had to walk up and down the rifle range screaming out "I AM A PUSSY AND A DISGRACE TO THE MARINE CORPS." This went on for about an hour. Every time he got in front of someone who qualified, he had to say he was sorry that he fucked up and was a useless piece of shit. It was a bad day for my brother Jack. His mind was at the point of breaking. His cheeks were wet with tears. Will we graduate from boot camp at 17, together like we planned, or will he kill himself tonight?

When our platoon got back to the barracks, all of the UNQ'S had to line up and scream out that they were a disgrace to themselves and to the Marines. The drill instructor wanted to kill all of them. "We don't need people who can't shoot in my Marine Corps," he said. We did not know if they would be killed. I would have to stop them from killing Jackie.

"What should we do with these maggots?" yelled the drill instructor? No one answered.

"What are we going to do with these fucking Maggots?" the drill instructor asked, as he stood in front of me.

"What?" He had asked again. If I didn't think of something, the instructors would kick and punch Jackie until he was almost dead. His mind would be gone for all times. The drill instructors would probably laugh about that for years to come. I had to think of something to save Jackie. I said, "I will beat my brother into the ground Sir."

A smile appeared on the drill instructors face, he was happy with that. One brother beating the shit out of the other, he was very happy with that and said with a smile, "Do it and make him bleed. Make him pay for fucking up my Marine Corps."

I said, "Yes Sir, Sir." I looked at Jackie and started to call him a pussy and a fuck up. He knew what was going to happen next. I punched him in the face and pushed him into the head. (That is a term used for the bathroom)

Growing up, we used to always fake a fight and we could make it look like we were killing each other. Friday and Saturday nights as kids in rockaway beach we would start a fight in front of the bars our father was in and we would get money to stop fighting by the drunks coming out. "Be good kids" they would say as they handed us a few quarters. Our punches were held back and our kicks look like they would hurt each other. We practiced judo, karate, and boxing almost every day. Both of us could take a punch, Jackie better than me. Many times growing up we would punch each other in the stomach to see who would go down first. Our bodies were like rocks.

As I was pushing Jackie, he slipped on the floor and cut his arm, which started to bleed. The drill instructors were listening from outside in the hallway. I told Jack to rub the blood on his face and to scream out "No more, stop! I am your brother! No more, please stop." I grabbed him, threw him out the door, and flipped him almost in front of the Son of God. "You fucking cry baby," I said, and kicked him again in the stomach and flipped him back into the Head. We practiced falling many times so I knew Jackie was not getting hurt. It looked good and it did fool the drill instructors. Jackie came staggering out of the Head, with his face covered with blood and tears in his eyes. Good thing he splashed his face with water when I threw him into the shower room. John was told to get in front of his bunk, and pray that God will have mercy on his soul and to be forgiven for fucking up. Also to thank God that the Son of God didn't have to dirty his own hands on a useless piece of puke like him.

The drill instructor looked at me and said, "Good Job, well done." You made the Marine Corps proud by taking care of your own shit bird. But you should have flushed that piece of shit down the toilet. I stood in front of the drill instructor and didn't say anything but, "Yes Sir, Sir." I knew tomorrow this would be forgotten and I would be back on the shit list with my drill instructors. He said that the gators weren't smiling tonight. But he didn't know that Jackie and I were.

I couldn't talk to Jackie that night because the lights were going out and also if I got caught talking to him, the drill instructors would kill me. We knew that we did a good job and no one was going to fuck with the Byrne boys. We just had to be careful not to let the drill instructors know that we could fake a fight.

One day, they did find out.

CHAPTER 6

GETTING IN SHAPE THE MARINE WAY

"You Maggots are Pogey Bait garbage!" (Pogey Bait is a term used in the Marine Corps for someone who is overweight, eats a lot of candy, and is out of shape.) "What did you do before coming here to my boot camp? You piece of shit. What did you do all day? Sit on your mommy's laps and suck on her tits? You are not even a man, you can't even do one pull up, you piece of garbage. How did you get into my Marine Corps, you overweight, do nothing, candy eating, piece of garbage? You will be doing sit-ups until you drop dead. You will get that weight off and make me proud on graduation day. If you cannot get it together, you will go to the motivation platoon. If my brother drill instructors don't get you motivated to get off your sorry fat asses and make us proud, then they will shoot you and leave your fat ass for the gators. Why do you think Parris Island is surrounded by water and those gators always look happy? Why? They know that some of you maggots are not up to being Marines and never will be. That is why Mr. Happy, the gator is licking his lips. Get it together girls or you will be his next meal!"

I think at that time, everyone wanted to do as many sit-ups, push-ups and anything else, that the Sons of God wanted us to do. At 17 years old, my brother Jackie and I were in good shape. Our bodies were like rocks but not our minds. We were brainwashed into believing everything the Gods told us. After listening to the drill instructor and starting to shake and sweat, thinking that we'd be gator bait, we'd force ourselves to do more.

Afterward we ran around the base shouting, "Left—right— left, Mommy and Daddy lying in bed, Momma rolled over and she said, feels good', the way to go, got to go, Marine Corps, all the way, every day, got to go, don't stop, never stop, got to go." That is just one of the many sounds that the platoon screamed out all day, every day. We ran around the base getting rid of our baby fat! drill instructors don't want any baby fat turds in their platoon. My brother Jackie and I got rid of our baby fat when we were babies. We were lean and mean before we got to the Marines.

We just don't know how much we will be pushed. What limits are the Marines looking for?

The drill instructors didn't think there were any limits to the strength of every recruit. They wanted us to be even harder than we were and harder we would get.

When Jackie and I were in our last year in high school, we were always running and exercising every day. We didn't let one day go by without doing some form of exercise. In gym class, we signed up for the Marine fitness program. This was a program that timed each exercise; there were five or six of them, each one had to be done in a number of minutes. The clock was always ticking. We both had no problems getting the minimum time and number for each exercise. But we wanted to and did the most repetitions with every exercise, every day. We had to be the best.

Our daily schedule went something like this:

Sit-ups: We had to do 60 in two minutes. I did 115 in two minutes.

Jackie did 100.

Pull-ups: We had to do 10.Jackie did 25.

I did 19.

Push-ups: We had to do 25. Jackie did 75.

I did 55 to 60.

Running all day, jumping jacks, squat jumps, squat thrust doing it easy was not our way. At 17, we could do it all.

The big week had finally come to our platoon. Most of the recruits were ready to be tested for the physical readiness test.

The week before the platoon was on the confidence course. We climbed a 20-foot structure that looks like a ladder, a high obstacle that we had to get over quickly. There was also a 100-foot rope that we had to go down, hand over hand across a large body of muddy water. It was about 10 to 15 feet above the water, or should I say a mud hole. Jackie and I had no trouble doing the rope climb or anything else that required climbing. We did all of this growing up and in high school, so we thought this was like playing a game. We did this rope climb in an L shape many times over the years. This was a game to us but the drill instructors would not let any recruit win even if they were impressed with the results. As we went down the rope Jackie and I made it look like we were having fun. The Sons of God saw this and told us to do it again.

"Yes Sir, Sir," we screamed together. Thinking of how proud the drill instructor would be of us, we climbed the rope, in an L shape, as fast as we could. Then I started down the 100-foot rope across the muddy water. I was first to go down while Jackie stood on the platform waiting his turn. The drill instructor screamed for me to stop. I did.

He then said, "Let go, you piece of shit." I couldn't believe what I heard and was about to tell him to go fuck yourself, but I was only thinking of that in my mind. To have those words come out of my mouth, I would be gone in a few minutes and the gators would be smiling. I had to drop into the mud, with all my clothes on, including my rifle. Then it was Jack's turn to drop. Jackie tried to make it to the end of the rope without dropping into the water. He dropped on land. The drill instructor got in his face and screamed "You fucking Maggot!" I should leave you in the mud hole and let the fucking pigs eat you. He told him to walk into the mud hole. He did that up to his neck and then was told to get on the rope again. The mud added another 15 pounds on to him. Jackie was told to drop again, from the highest point. No matter how you drop into the mud, you will have mud from your hair to your toes. We then sat there in the sun until everything was dried. We were told to run back to the barracks and get clean. It took us until the lights were going out before we were done.

Some days they might tell us that they were proud of us. After a week in boot camp, the drill instructors were like our parents we wanted to and had to please them. In a few days, we were going to be logged into the company's books. Jackie and I were ready to show them what we could do.

The final count to be recorded was upon us. For years, I have done sit-ups until it hurt. Whenever we fucked up, the drill instructor would hit Jackie or me. They would punch us in the stomach as hard as they could and we bent over and made a sound like they were hurting us. This started from the first day in boot camp. One night before lights went out; we were given 15 minutes of free time. (To write letters, do more exercises or shine our shoes.) It was crazy, but we always did some form of exercise. Jackie and I made a big mistake that night. We bet a few of the guys in the platoon a dollar, that they could not double us over by punching us in the stomach. We won a few dollars, but in the long run, we lost to the Sons of God. Jackie got hit first, won his dollar and walked away. The senior drill instructor heard someone say hit Jerry harder. He turned from what he was doing to see me standing, after one of the guys punched me, as hard as he could in the stomach. I was smiling and said, "Is that the best you got?" Sit-ups paid off for me that night.

The next day as we were marching, I made a mistake and the senior drill instructor came over screaming in my face. "You fucking maggot, get it together." He then went to punch me in the stomach and like I always do when he did this, I bent down from my waist and made a sound like he was hurting me. I got punched in the face and thought that one of my teeth had fallen out. He said, "That was for smiling, maggot. Don't ever try to put one over on your drill instructors because we will feed you to the gators."

Later in the week, the counting began.

Each group had two people counting the number of repetitions of each exercise that we had to do. The guys couldn't believe it when I did 115 sit-ups in two minutes. When the drill instructor came over to get the count he said, "Bull shit," when they told him the number.

He said, "You lying scrum shits." No one had ever done that many before. He looked at me and said, "Do it again, and this time I will be doing the counting. If you don't get the same number I will kill you." There was no reason for me to think that he wouldn't do me in. But I didn't care because in my mind I could do it again, after only a few minutes of rest.

The drill Instructor called a few of the other drill instructors over to witness this count. I think that he knew I could do it again, but he wanted some of the others to see it also. I think he wanted to take the credit for having someone in his platoon taking first place for doing sit-ups.

The drill instructor said, "On my count, go." With that, I started to do as many as I could in two minutes. I did 115 sit-ups. I was hoping for 120 sit-ups today but maybe another day. My drill instructor said to the other drill instructors, "Can any of your turds beat that?" I had a good feeling for a while even thought my instructor did not say I did well. We wouldn't get any pats on the ass until graduation day.

When it came to pull-up's Jackie had it over the rest of the platoon by doing 25 or 30. The drill instructors did the count, but another recruit from another platoon did 10 more than Jackie. Since we were always getting punched around by the drill instructors almost every day I think they were impressed by how we did. They gave us a break, for the rest of the day. We only had to run 3 miles, instead of 4.

The Pogey Bait Marines who made the drill instructors look bad because they couldn't come close to doing what the rest of the platoon did had to run the extra 2 miles. There were more than just a few of them that passed out and fell to the ground, from running around the field. The rest of the platoon stood in formation to watch the fatties run. The ones that fell to the ground were taken to the hospital to be checked out, some did not return to our platoon. We were told that the gators were happy that night.

The drill instructors were Gods to be believed. We never knew if the dropouts went to the gators or not. We were all thankful that it was not us. The Marines didn't want any half assed, make-believe recruits; only the best will graduate from Parris Island.

After one somewhat happy day for Jackie and I, the battle for graduation started again at five the following morning. It didn't take long for Jackie and I to fall off the high pedestal that we were on, but we were happy to be on it for one day.

The only ones that will always be on a pedestal will be the drill instructors. No recruit will ever knock them off. They will be remembered longer than all the prophets.

CHAPTER 7

A SAD DAY FOR THE WORLD

Give me your—left—right—left, right—left—right, all day long, it never ends. The drill instructor screams as loud as he can and your foot had better be on the left or right when they say left or right. The Marine Corps marching machine, close order drill in boot camp, is taught to develop teamwork and instant obedience to a command. My brother Jackie and I received many kicks and punches for the last 10 weeks. It was not easy being twins in the same platoon in boot camp. When the drill instructor said, "About face, to the rear, ya," every recruit (we were not Marines yet) makes a complete turn and marches the opposite way. I failed some days to be as fast as the other marchers. The Gods came over to me and pushed me to the ground.

They screamed, "You dumb shit, kiss the ground that you are walking on." The two guys to my left and right, started to laugh. My brother Jackie was one of them.

They had to run around the parade ground, screaming, "Marines don't laugh, left—right—left. Marines don't smile, left—right—left." This went on for a couple of hours. They had to be louder than the drill instructors, so that they could be heard over the loud sounds that the other platoons were making. I still don't know my left foot from my right. Two weeks to go, I will get it together. I have to get it together and Jackie had to as well or we would be killed. If he fucks up then I will get a beating. I screwed up many times and Jackie had to endure the kicks and punches. I told Jackie that I fucked up on purpose, so he can get punched around. It was pay back for all the times that he ate all the candy and ice cream as kids and I didn't get any. I had to watch myself that I did the right things most of the time so I wouldn't get a beating also. We couldn't figure out the mind of the drill instructors. Marine Corps boot camp would soon be over, and we will be proud to be Marines, if the drill instructors, which are like the Sons of God, didn't kill us before graduation day, which would be in two weeks. The drill instructors wanted everyone in the grandstands to know how great they are when we are marching by and that they are the ones that got us to look sharp, in step and jumping at the sound of the drill instructors voice. We were told many times that we would get shot and dumped in the water that surrounds Parris Island and would be eaten by the alligators if we can't get it together for graduation. There will be no fuck up's on graduation day. We all hoped that God was on our side and guides us to be in step. My parents and sister are coming down to see their angels and to hear the Commanding Officer say, "Welcome Marines, you are now one of the few and proud, congratulations."

After hours on the parade ground in the morning, we went to lunch. Fifteen minutes to get your food, eat and be outside in formation eyes looking straight ahead. The drill instructors always changed their position around lunchtime. They all took turns to drill us or run us into the ground, which gave them a few hours to eat and to rest up. In the beginning of Boot Camp, Jackie and I thought that they did

55

the same things as the rest of us at the same time. Running, marching and eating at times, we couldn't keep up with them but then again there were three of them. When you are so scared to look at them and your eyes are always straight ahead, it is easy to be misled. At this point, I think we were completely brainwashed. Two weeks to go.

At 12: o'clock we were back doing what the drill instructors wanted and getting better with every step. Jackie or I didn't get hit too many times in the morning. Maybe we were lucky that they didn't see us when we fucked up or maybe we were getting better. The instructor sees every move and a misstep stands out immediately. There are 70 to 80 men in formation lined up and marching, making turns, left and right and to the rear, and doing it all as one. Precision that is seen as unbelievable by those looking on. Only then can we be proud of our movement and ourselves.

The noise was loud with four hundred or more recruits on the parade grounds, together in step the way we were trained to do. The drill instructors yelled as loud as they could at the recruits as we marched to stay in step. Left, right, left, keep in line, the sounds would wake up the dead. The noise of the movement wouldn't bother someone watching if they were deaf, others hold your ears. There were more than four hundred Marine privates, on the field, doing the right thing so that they could graduate on time. There is always one recruit who does not make it to the end to graduate from his original platoon and they are usually put back to another platoon. We did not know about that until after graduation. We thought that they took the recruits that were not motivated out back and shot them. I don't know what I would have done to myself if they put me back. That would mean a few more weeks in hell. Mentally it would be a wipe out. This is something that everyone thinks about within a few days of getting to Parris Island S.C. Marine Corps boot camp.

This looks like another day in hell. Left—right—left, keep it together, there were no resting and anyone who says that they are tired after lunch will not get lunch the next day. The Sons of God are smart enough, that they don't tell the recruit that he can't have lunch (due to congressional investigations at times) but does say, he only had one minute to get his food, eat and be outside the mess hall at attention in formation, when the drill instructors walks out of the building. Pray to God that that the private is not late. Their stopwatch is always out.

This marching has been going on for weeks. At night it was hard to sleep at times, because all you hear inside your head is, left, right, left, two weeks to go. Even in your dreams, the drill instructors face is in yours. Wakening up in a sweat is not uncommon at night.

Everything around us stopped.

It was 12:45 pm. We were told to stop. There was no movement on the Parade grounds. No sound! No marching and everyone standing at attention. We couldn't believe this was happening. No sounds from anywhere and the drill instructors with tears in their eyes and their heads shaking, from side to side were down and we didn't know what was going on. No one in formation moved or looked around, waiting to be told something. What was happening? Ten weeks in boot camp and no one had seen anything like this before.

After ten minutes, the drill instructors came over to the Platoon, all three of them, at the same time. They walked up and down the lines and said, "Be ready for war." This is a sad, sad, day for the United States of America. They left us standing at attention. What the fuck happened. No one was telling us. We were not allowed newspapers, radios or television while in boot camp.

One private from our platoon was caught with a newspaper and a doughnut tucked inside of his shirt a few days after getting to boot camp. He was made to sit inside a garbage can, with the cover on it and to scream repeatedly, "I am a fuckin pig and should die." The drill instructor then kicked the can over and started to roll it, from one end of the squad bay to the other, while everyone in the platoon had to hit the side of the can and call the private in the can a fat fucking pig. If the private didn't think he was going to die at that time, there would have to be something wrong with him. With all the things that Jackie and I did wrong, it never came to that. Since day one there were many punches in our face and stomach and screaming that we were pieces of shit and should not be in the Marine Corps. At times, the tears would flow, but we would never let the drill instructors see wet eyes.

We were told to march back to the barracks and not make a sound. Stay in front of your rack and don't move. "What the

Fuck was going on?" we whispered to each other. Praying that the drill instructors didn't see our lips move. Less than two weeks to graduation day and now this. Why did the drill instructors say "it was a sad, sad, day for all of us?"

We all waited, we had no choice but to wait. We may all go off to die in a war, but there was no war going on when Jackie and I got into boot camp.

An hour went by and then the senior drill instructor walked into the barrack, tears in his eyes. A few minutes later, the other drill instructors stood next to him. Their heads were down and they demanded that we all put our heads down and pray. Pray that God will have mercy on us. I was thinking get to the fucking point, what was going on. Why should we be scared when we were almost Marines? We don't fear anyone except the drill instructors. I hope they cannot read my mind now or I would probably die immediately. The way they were looking, I thought that they wanted to kill someone. I hope it is not one of us.

The senior drill instructor started to speak and said, "Today a great man has been killed." We don't have all the information as of now. A fucking scumbag shot and killed our Commander in Chief. A fucking Russian communist pig," he said over and over. "Get ready to go to war. I am ready and you maggots are almost ready." He wouldn't call us Marines until we graduated.

Today was Friday, November 22, 1963, and at 12:29 P.M. the 35th President of the United States of America, John F. Kennedy, was shot in Texas by Lee Harvey Oswald. Shot in the head while waving to the people. The assassination was on everyone mind. Are we going to war? How many people were killed, with the president? Was his wife killed? Many questions and none of them can be answered by the recruit next to you. No one had a radio or a newspaper. For now, we can only turn the facts that we know of around in circles. Saying the same thing over and over, and making up more stories as the day goes on. It would be like what the news media does today with a story that they know nothing about. It would be a couple of days before we found out the rest of the story about the assassination.

One drill instructor told us a couple of days later that a former Marine, by the name of Lee Harvey Oswald, who defected to the Soviet Union and became a communist and then returned to the United States to kill our president. Some of the recruits wanted to know what the Soviet Union was. The drill instructor were too wiped out to yell at them today for being stupid and told us all that it was another name for Russia. Almost 50 years later, the conspiracy theories are still going around, even more now then back in 1963. Did President Johnson do it? Were there two assassins firing their rifles at the same time? Did Kennedy's wife have something to with it? (Kennedy had many girls coming into the White house for sex every week.) Hundreds of books have been written about Kennedy, many investigations were held about the killing, and there were still no answers. The one book that comes close to the real story in my view is the Anxious Assassins by Keith Laufenberg. Someday the truth will come out, when there is enough money given to those with the information. The secret of the third bullet is still a question to be answered and one of the great mysteries of our time.

For a few days after this talk and information that was given to us, there was a change in the drill instructors voices. They seemed to be lower than usual. Not as mean, their emotions seemed to be drained, for their leader was dead, our leader as well but the training must go on. We are still maggots.

5:00 A.M. in the morning and the sun was hiding in the clouds; we were all running and running, up the hill and down the hill. The sweat pouring off us, the legs are tired but the Sons of God do not care if we are worn out, we have to be ready. The drill instructor said to run as fast as we could until 6:00 a.m. each and every morning until graduation day and we can't fail. This is the start of our day. There is no other platoon out running until 6:00 a.m. The rest of the day is running, doing push-ups, sit-ups and more marching. Left—right—left, for twelve more hours.

We will look good for our President, when he looks down from heaven at us, and gives us his blessing. To the drill instructors, Kennedy was a God but at 17 years old, I didn't know much about him. I only knew that he was the first Catholic president. (After reading many books years later about President Kennedy, I did learn about him.) We must be ready, we will be ready. War may be around the corner waiting for us. The thing that got me to keep running every morning was the smell of bacon and eggs and the thought of getting a large plate of SOS. (SOS is shit on a shingle, which is ground up beef, mixed with flour, in a gravy-like sauce.) Jackie and I couldn't wait to have breakfast every morning while in the Marine Corps. I guess it was time for all of us to put a few pounds on, to fill out the uniform on graduation day. After running for an hour we went right to the mess hall, it doesn't get much better than that. The final weeks are near and I guess the drill instructors wanted everyone to eat as much as they could. But if the food goes on your plate every last piece must be eaten. The Instructors are watching you like a hawk to see that there is not anything left on the plate. If they see you throwing any food out from your plate you will get a beating. They may even have you eat out of the garbage cans, until you vomit even if it is close to graduation day. There is a sign in the Marine Corps Mess Hall "Take all you want, but eat all you take." Do not break that law.

Graduation day has finally come. We are in the Marine Corps uniform looking unbeatable and great. After doing thousands of sit-ups, hundreds of push-ups and weeks of close order drilling, our confidence is at an all-time high. We are almost Marines, we have to wait for the command "pass in review" to be given by the command officer of the base. Before the admiring eyes of family and friends, our platoon # 272, marches together for the last time. All of us in the platoon marching with our shoulders back, chest out, as proud as any peacock could ever be.

One thing you will not see is a smile on any recruits face, not yet anyway, until we get the official word. We are Marines. We made it past the Commanding offices, in step and no one fucked up. The drill instructors were proud and they even said hello to our families, which we couldn't believe. Some of them came over to Jackie and me and said, "A job well done." The pain and bruises from the kicks and punches went away after time and boot camp is now over for us but it will be forever in our nightmares.

Every Marine has a story to tell about Boot Camp, and when they are telling the story, it feels like it was happening yesterday. It is never forgotten and the title was earned by all who graduated.

THE TITLE OF UNITED STATES MARINES WILL BE WITH US FOREVER

SEPTEMBER 18, 1963 TO DECEMBER 6, 1963

OUR DAYS IN HELL WERE NOW OVER SO WE THOUGHT

VIETNAM WAS COMING SOON

CHAPTER 8

THE FIGHT

It was a great day. Jackie and I are now real Marines. A long
day of tension; both of us praying that we didn't fuck up
while marching in front of our parents or the Commanding
General of the Marine Corps. Our mother, father, and little
sister were impressed to see their angels looking like men
instead of the children we were just a few months before.
We went to the mess hall for the first time on our own and
ate as much as we wanted without being told to eat fast. The
quality of the food was of high standards and my parents
and sister ate enough to keep them happy for the day. Our
father had a couple of steaks and a baked potato.

He said, "This is great that they serve you guys this much
food every day." After lunch, we went to the PX (Post
Exchange, which is a retail store on the base) to get my
father a few cartons of cigarettes at one dollar a carton.
Jackie or I didn't start smoking for another couple of
months, sometime in March or April 1964. We walked
around the base looking at the old barrack complexes that
were still in use today. We showed them the swimming pool
and gym. Our father liked the idea that the pool and gym
could be used at any time. Not to be used by recruits but
only those Marines stationed at Parris Island. Our parents
spoke to the drill instructors thinking that they were good to
us and took care of us. We told our parents when we get

home that the truth will be known. We will never forget the first mail call or the months following it.

It was time to call it a day, to go back to the barracks and pack up all of our belongings. The platoon was going to Camp Geiger, North Carolina in the morning.

We were all hanging around the barracks, proud of ourselves that we made it. We started to talk about the next step in our new life as real Marines, when someone said we could get away with more things. The sergeants won't be on our ass all day.

I said, "We got away with a lot in boot camp that the drill instructors didn't know about."

Jackie said, "We tricked the scumbags a couple of times." With those words, everyone looked around to see if the drill instructors were in the area, thank God that they were inside reading or drinking. They too had a few days off for doing a good job getting us ready for the big day. They were still near but not breaking anyone's chops. We don't know what they would do if they found out about me and Jackie faking a fight. We did graduate, but are still under their control for another day, or until we get on the bus the next morning. Everyone around us wanted to know how we tricked them.

Jackie and I stood up and said, "We will show you."

We went into the area where we worked out and a few of the other Marines followed us. As Jackie was standing in front of me, I punched him as fast as I could in the mouth. He fell back and kicked me on the side of my face, then punched me in the stomach. Our hands were fast and as we punched and blocked each other punches, the drill instructors came out of their headquarters and were looking at us from the corner of the room. I grabbed Jackie, flipped him over my shoulder, and jumped on his chest. He screamed in pain. He jumped off the floor, reached toward my legs, and pushed me back into a wall. He jumped up and put both feet into my chest, leaned back and flipped me over his head and I landed in the next room. When I landed I yelled, "That hurt you fucking, UNQ. Fuck. I am going to kill you, even if you are my fucking brother." I punched him about twenty times in the ribs. He yelled, "I am your brother why are you doing this to me?" I grabbed his hand, flipped him over my shoulder, and kicked him again while he was going down.

Jackie said, "Please stop, you won. Stop, no more please."

I stepped back and said, "Well, I won, you piece of shit," I kicked him again in the stomach, with that he started to cry. I reached over to his shoulders and pulled him toward me; I started to knee him about five times, in the stomach, and then threw him on the floor.

I said, "Did you have enough?" Keep crying you fucking crybaby. He got up from the ground very quick, into a fighting stand, and then we smiled at each other and shook hands. I turned to the guys around us and said, "That is how we tricked the drill instructors." Just like the stuntmen in the movies; neither of us were hurt or in pain. The guys couldn't believe it. We started to laugh and said we did this for years; we always made it look good. We took turns on who would win. The laughter stopped, as our eyes looked into the eyes, of the Son of God, who witnessed the fight at the rifle range.

If looks could kill, there would be two dead Marines on the floor of the workout area. We were still under the drill instructors control and we didn't know if they could put us back for tricking them. We did graduated this morning and there were no more yelling or hitting any of the recruits all day. The senior drill instructor came over to us and said that was very impressive. "You guys made all those moves look real."

I said, "Yes Sir, Sir." When the last word came out of my mouth, the drill instructor went to punch me in the stomach, but didn't, he stopped an inch from making contact with my stomach. Why he didn't go after Jackie, I don't know?

He said, "You guys are Marines now, we don't hit after boot camp. You learned what we wanted to teach you, now you are out of here. I never saw anything like that, you put one over on us and I have to say it was a good one. You should both be fighters," he said, "Don't fuck up and you will be good Marines." Don't teach any new recruits those moves, or "I will be looking for you." He said, "I still can't believe how real that was. Good job, Marines, Semper Fi. Go to bed, tomorrow will be a long day."

"Yes Sir, Sir." We still didn't smile.

We couldn't believe he said that to us. For the rest of the night, we slept with one eye open for fear that the drill instructor would change his mind about hitting.

CHAPTER 9

CAMP GEIGER—CAMP LEJEUNE

The sun was shining bright outside at 0530, when the lights came on in the barracks. Last day for all of us in boot camp and we were all happy to be getting out of Parris Island. The drill instructors were not screaming for us to get up. In fact they came in and said that the buses would be out front at 0800, (8:00 a.m.) If you miss the bus, you will be staying a few more months at Parris Island. They did have a smile on their faces. Get something to eat and be ready to leave. Jackie and I ran to the mess hall and ate bacon and eggs and our favorite meal, SOS, (shit on the shingle) for an hour, with three cups of coffee, without anyone telling us to hurry up. What a difference a day makes.

"We raced back to get our bags," I told Jackie, "I am going to kick him off the bus, I am the best."

He said, "Don't fuck with me, I am a Marine." I told him he was a pussy and he will never make it in my Marine Corps. We have said that to each other many times over the years since boot camp. No one was taking any chances on missing the bus. At 0730, the whole platoon, number 272, had their sea bag in front of them, packed with everything that they owned and lined up at the bus stop. Thirty minutes earlier than we were told to be there, no one wanted to stay longer then we had to in Parris Island.

We were all excited and happy to be leaving this base. No one wanted to be late. The buses were on time and everyone placed their bag in the storage area on the bus, and then boarded. The drill instructors said their goodbyes and shook our hands, as we entered the bus to get our seats. At 0815, we were on our way to Camp Geiger, North Carolina. The bus, filled with new recruits, left Parris Island through the main gate, we all screamed at the same time. "Fuck you, we're out of here!" Now we all felt safe from the hands of the drill instructors. At our next training camp, after traveling a few hundred miles, and five hours later, we entered a new main gate and were happy to leave the old one behind. We would all be getting more training for combat, learning to kill the enemy before they kill us. We are United States Marines, "don't fuck with us."

Checking into Camp Geiger didn't have all the screaming and pushing like Parris Island did. In fact, as we got off the bus, we were told by a sergeant to go into the barracks and get yourself a wall locker and bunk, go to the mess hall and eat and fall out tomorrow morning at 0800 to start your day in training.

Two hundred and fifty new Marines ready to kick ass were assigned to Company "E," First Battalion, First Infantry Training Regiment. We were just out of boot camp and in need of training now. This will be only for a few more days until we get our papers for leave, thirty days at home, or wherever we wanted to go and then we would be back, for weapons and infantry training.

These next few days were just to get our papers and schedules in order. The time for training will be in January, when we got back from a well-deserved leave. We needed the time off for our minds to become sane again, if that were possible after boot camp.

After the big surprise of coming home, smiling both of us started to unpack our sea bag, we never told my mother and father what day we would be coming. Jackie and I tried to tell our parents what it was really like at Parris Island while we were eating the bacon and eggs that my mother always made for us. Since we didn't have any bruises on our face and looked to be in good shape, we were both 175 pounds and as hard as rocks, our stories fell on deft ears. After my parents had a meeting and talked with the drill instructors, at the parade grounds only a few weeks ago, it would be hard for them, or anyone to believe how vicious and violent these men in their dress blues and smiles, were to new recruits, especially twins.

We enjoyed our 30 days of freedom by seeing our friends from high school and going to a couple of parties. While home on leave, we went back to our high school to see our former teachers. One teacher always had us standing in line without talking every day after lunch, waiting for the doors to open into his classroom. They couldn't believe how much we had changed. We didn't think we did after being away for only six months. We were standing proud in front of the class, in our new uniforms, with spit-shine shoes and medals pined to our shirts. Many questions on boot camp were answered as we told the guys that we were in school with only months before that, they would never have what it takes to be Marines. We were hoping that a couple of guys that we didn't like would sign up after high school. Pay back is a bitch.

Jackie and I made it to the World's Fair in 1964, and took a couple of girls from the neighborhood with us. I didn't have much money in my pockets, but Jackie was buying the girls food and drinks with no problems paying for it. I didn't find out until months later that he took money from a box that I had in my dresser at home. I had saved a few dollars every week over the years and had a few hundred dollars. I did beat the shit out of him and wouldn't talk to him for weeks. I didn't get the money back. I was pissed and had to find a way to get him back. I found a way to get him back months later when we came home on a weekend. Late on a Saturday night while leaving Manhattan, he didn't have any tokens for the train ride in his pockets and had to wait on line to buy them. The train was coming into the station, so I told him I would hold the doors open for him until he can get on the train. I waited until he was almost near the doors of the train and then I let the doors close in his face. I waved good-bye. It took him more than a few hours to get home. Not many trains run at that time in the morning. Pay back is a bitch.

Because of the parking problems, it was always easier for us to take a taxi or train while going into the city when we were home on the weekend.

We had a great time for thirty days at home then it was back to Camp Geiger for four weeks of weapons training. Jackie and I tried to master the skills that were taught us, but to really master the training a Marine needs to be in combat. Like a boxer, you can't learn to fight by reading a book. Most Marines are proud of the training that they received and many will never forget it, proud to be Marines and the mindset to be the best. It is a challenge to be in the Marines and Jackie and I were always up for the part. That feeling would last for the rest of our lives.

At Camp Geiger, we still did physical training (PT) every day but not like boot camp. We did field trips at night, playing war games in the wooded area around the base, walked for miles in the rain and still had to be up at 5:00 a.m. A few times a week we had inspections on all our equipment. If the Marine didn't pass inspections, he would have to stay on base all weekend and do mess duty or guard duty.

Our days were filled with many things to learn. Map reading and then finding a given location using a map. Throwing hand grenades, (there is always someone in the group, who will get nervous while pulling the pin, which will arm the grenade and then drop the grenade next to them.) You have about five seconds before it explodes. Thank God that no one got killed in my group. We also learned to use flamethrowers, mortars and machine guns. I carried the M79 grenade launcher, which looked like a sawed–off shotgun. It could hurl a grenade a few hundred yards. I also carried the M14 rifle and a 45-caliber pistol.

After four or five weeks we were told that it is time to move on to a new base for more activity. We didn't have a choice.

It was time to travel around the world with the best fighting machine in the world.

Jackie and I were assigned to Company "H," 2nd battalion, 2nd Marines in Camp Lejeune, North Carolina. They were separating us, same company but different platoons. I went to the 2nd platoon and Jackie to the 1st or Weapons platoon, at the other end of the building, only a few yards from where I was. We stayed together for more than a year.

We were in and out of Camp Lejeune for the next two years, packing up our gear and going to other countries for war games. In four years, we went to many places around the world. We both went to the Caribbean islands for three months, not for a vacation, or fun, but to train in the heat, and rain. We had a training base on the island of Vieques, Puerto Rico, for amphibious exercise, and simulated war games. Marines jumping out of the landing crafts that carried us near the shore. We were all running in waist deep water, with all of our field equipment, clothes and weapons getting wet. This was done many times in the months ahead. There were also hours spent cleaning up the sand and water from our gear. We also went to many of the countries in the Caribbean for liberty and to spend our ninety dollars a month, in the bars near the docks, to help the local economy. Marines were the backup force for any country that needed the power of the United States, anywhere in the Caribbean Islands. As far as going on tours, there were not many that we wanted to go on. Many of us would usually end up in the nearest bar a few hundred yards away from the ships that were transporting us.

One night, close to the base at our training camp, a few Marines went into the nearest town to get something to eat, drink and dance with the local girls. One Marine stayed in town drinking, while the others headed back early to the base for the night. The next morning the Marine that stayed behind was found by the local police in a gully, with both arms cut and almost dead. We were on the range that day shooting weapons and one of the guys said, "Let's go into the town tonight and let them know that they can't fuck with the Marines." We went to the nearest bar from where the Marine was found and wanted to know what happened.

The bar owner said, "Fuck you, get out." Someone threw a chair into the mirrored wall behind the barkeeper. The rest of us took chairs and threw them into the front windows. One of the Marines said the MP'S were coming. Outside we saw lights and heard the sounds of dogs in the distance. After telling everyone in the bar to go fuck your-selves and that we will return, we all ran back to the base. I undressed and just got into bed, around 3:00 a.m. before the lights came on. We all had to stand at attention outside the barracks, while the police chief and others from the town walked in front of us. They couldn't pick anyone out of the crowd. We all had white shirts and briefs on and we were all around the same weight. The commanding officer of the base told us to stay at attention until the police left. After a few minutes, the officer said it wasn't right for us to take action on our own; someone could have been killed.

"But enough of that," he said, "I am proud of you all, for doing what Marines do best. Don't fuck with the Marine

Corps."

After returning to the States, for a few months, we packed up and shipped out for Spain, twice. An operation called, Steel Pike, 1 and 2, for training with about 1500 Marines and Allied forces for an Amphibious landing on the island of Sardinia in July, 1965.

There were many days of fun time after the landing. We went to many ports around the Mediterranean countries. I actually went on a sightseeing tour of Italy for a week. The tour of Italy for a week only cost me $25, which included a hotel room and dinner in four or five cities. Thank you Uncle Sam, one of the few things that I would remember with a smile on my face after four years of military life. Years later, going back to Italy for a few weeks with my wife cost me thousands of dollars. I couldn't get Uncle Sam to foot the bill this time.

After six months of travelling around the Mediterranean Islands, on and off the ship in many ports, drinking and fighting, showing everyone how tough Marines were, H Company, 2/2, headed back to the States. I am really surprised that many of us didn't get thrown in jail in these other countries. One day when I was walking around the streets of Italy, with five or six Marines, someone from another group of Marines yelled that Marines were in trouble. We ran to the nightclub up the block and saw that an Italian policeman had his pistol out and was telling the Marines, to get out of the club. I pushed my way up near the front and yelled, "Fuck you," you can only shoot one of us before the Marines kill you. And we will kill you. I must have had a few drinks in me, to say that. There were two more cops in the back of the club standing there surrounded by a hundred Marines. The cop with the pistol pointing at the Marine, decided to put it away, said, it was a misunderstanding, and put his hand out to shake hands. He was smart enough to understand; that he would have been killed and we would have been all put in jail.

Back in the United States at Camp Lejeune, we had our many inspections of our wall and footlockers and of course, we practiced war games in the field three days a week. After doing this every week, all we wanted was to go somewhere away from the base for the weekend. Jackie and I would just pick a town and go or get a ride too New York City. We would travel seventeen hours by car on a Friday night to spend Saturday night in Manhattan. Sunday afternoon we would try to get a ride back to the base, from 42nd street and 8th Ave. This happened many times in four years and Jackie and I never thought about getting robbed while traveling by car.

We were lucky. In Manhattan, we never told the group of people or girls that we both knew that we were twins. They would always say you look different have you lost weight, or gained weight. There were many weekends that one of us would have to stay on the base. We had a lot of stories to tell any girls that we met and they believed us. We were the ones buying drinks so they put up with us.

We were told one day, that the Commanding General of the base is going to do a walk though of our company in a few days. The officers and every Sergeant went into a panic. Start cleaning this place up, top to bottom all day every day, inside and out. We don't want to see any dust on anything. After the platoon cleaned for hours the sergeants came into the barracks' with buckets of soapy water, threw it around the floor and said clean it again. Everyone was afraid of the General, everyone except my brother Dennis.

Dennis went into the Marines about six months after Jackie and me. He was a private.

The big day came and we all had our uniforms cleaned and pressed, shoes shined, equipment cleaned and a quarter, would bounce on our beds to show, how tight the blankets were pulled. We were better than ever.

The General walked into our barracks, where everyone was waiting and standing at attention, no talking and fear of not passing this inspection on our minds. The General stood in front of the first Marine in the barrack and then side stepped to the next Marine. The General had many officers and platoon sergeants alongside of him, as he went down the line for the inspection. As the General moved from one Marine to the next, the previous Marine had a new officer in front of him. It was a long line and the tension was high. The Colonel, Major, Captain, Lieutenant and company personnel standing in front of a Marine to make sure he had everything done right according to the Marine Corps? Standing as stiff as a board, eyes straight ahead, I get a command "At ease Marine."

Standing in front of me is my brother Dennis, Captain Bars on his uniform, telling me that he was proud of his younger brother being in the Marine Corps. All I could say was, "Yes Sir, thank you Sir." This took balls, because he is only a private and his barracks is only a few yards away on the other side of the field.

The captain of my company came over to me after the General and Dennis left and said, "I didn't know you had a brother who was a captain in the Marines."

I wanted to say, "Neither did I Sir."

He said, "Where is he stationed?"

I said, "I didn't talk to my brother for a few years and didn't know where he was stationed Sir."

Thank God he only said, "Ok," and moved on to his quarters, and got ready for lunch.

I saw Dennis later that day; he was now a lieutenant, dressed as the officer of the day. He didn't care about getting caught. That was the way he was.

One Saturday morning, Jackie and a few friends were playing cards on his bunk after breakfast. I came over to his platoon and we talked about this wiseass Marine that thought it was funny to grab someone's food off their plate as he walked by them. Jackie came up with an idea. We got a box of donuts and left two of them in the box, then took the box outside and everyone around us pissed on them. Jackie left them in the sun to dry, on the side of the building for a few hours. He knew this guy would come around later in the day. After the donuts were dry, he took them inside and left them on the end of his rack. Jackie saw the Marine walking toward him and the other guys and started to eat one of the donuts that were not in the box. The guy walked fast by Jackie rack, grabbed the box, with the two donuts and ate them as fast as he could. He was laughing and said these were good. Jackie said, "Smell the box." The guy was sick for weeks, every time Jackie or I passed him in the barracks, we would say, "Smell the box," and he would get sick all over again. He never grabbed anyone's food again.

One thing Jackie and I did every year before and after we were in the Marines, were to get together on our birthday, December 10th. We would both say that we were sick, the day before our birthday, in Camp Lejeune, going to the doctors, (Sick-Bay) for stomach problems. The medical officer would give us a note to keep off our feet for a few days. Since we were in different location, no one ever found out. We would go to the club on base and drink and eat all day. We would really be sick the next day, a hangover. That would give us another day off from doing anything, so we could stay in bed all day.

After two years, the Marines asked me what duty station, would I like to go to for the next two years, since I had a four-year commitment? I picked the Brooklyn Navy Yard in New York, thinking that would be great for the weekends. I would be happy with that. Being stationed close to home, I even though of going back to school at night. The Marines said that would be too good for you, we are going to send you to Vietnam. I said, "Fuck it, I will go." I didn't have a choice and I didn't know where Vietnam was. The war only started for the Marines in 1965.It seemed that everyone in the platoon got the same orders, 13 months in Vietnam. I went to California first for a month, to train running up and down hills all day. I guess the Marine Corps knew what it was doing because in Vietnam we had to walk across rice patties and small rivers most of the time. Where are the hills? Jackie did not get his orders yet; he was staying in the states for now.

One weekend while in California a group of us decided to go into Mexico and have some fun. Since Tijuana is a short distance away, it seems to be a good idea. A dirty filthy place across the border, but we would have to go and get a few drinks and see the entertainment that the area was noted for. After a few hours of drinking in one place, I had to go to the men's room for a quick visit. While I was in there, a couple of Mexicans came in and said that the Marines didn't pay enough for their drinks. Now they have to pay more and give a few dollars back to the bar.

I said, "Ok, that is fair, we don't want any trouble." When I went back inside where the guys were, I said that the Mexicans were going to fuck us if we don't pay more. I said, "I am going to pick up a chair and throw it toward the bar and then we all run out without paying for anything." They liked that idea and we did it. The five of us jumped into a taxi just down the block from the bar and was on our way back to the base before anyone could stop us. Fuck the Mexicans.

Next stop—vacation in Vietnam.

CHAPTER 10

VIETNAM 1966

I left the shores of California toward the end of January 1966 on a Merchant Marine Ship, for 30 to 40 days being transported to a war zone. That is what they told us. Looking at the crewmates on the ship you wouldn't know it. In fact, anyone looking at the ship would think they were going on a cruise around the islands. The crew at times had beach chairs and coolers on the upper decks, listening to the radio or reading books. Some were smoking and drinking, looking across the large body of water with not a care in the world. Going to war? Be ready, that's what we were told. It didn't feel like a war zone, but then again we were on a ship in the middle of the Pacific Ocean. Going to Vietnam? Maybe this was going to be a vacation for us. But Marines don't get vacations in a war zone. But that is the impression we got. No one was breaking our balls and we were taking it easy. I did PT (physical training) in the morning, had something to eat and enjoyed the rest of the day. The ship had new movies that we watched almost every night. The food was always good, many bacon and egg and steak sandwiches. All we could eat three times a day. We were all putting on weight and getting fat. We were enjoying the good life most of the time. Little did we know that we would all be 20 to 40lbs. lighter after our tour of duty?

Tour of duty, that's the title the Marine Corps, gave for the 13 months "in country." Who was the fuck that thought of a term like that, someone maybe going to the Caribbean island or as a joke for those going to Vietnam? A tour of duty for over a year, sightseeing tours walking around the country side, in rice patties, going into hidden tunnels, caves and getting shot at. I could do without it. There were tunnels that went for miles, deep underground and large enough for jeeps and one hundred bed hospitals. Most of all, people who didn't like us. Going to war? The crewmembers from the ship were over in Vietnam, just a few months ago so how bad can going to war be. They all came back and all of them looked happy. They don't seem to be concerned. Maybe it is because as I found out later that the crew never leaves the ship and the ship stays out a few thousand yards from the shore, once it gets to Vietnam. Marines are usually the first to land, first to fight. I think the ship docked in Chu Lai harbor in the beginning of March. The ship stayed out in the harbor and the crew did stay on the ship. The Marines were transported to land in small boats. I was ready to return to the States a few hours after we docked as the Commanding Officer of the ship said "good luck" to all of us.

As the ship was entering the harbor, there was an explosion and then a fire in the engine room. The officers never told us what happened. Since we were in a combat zone, the Marines thought that we were being attacked, that someone bombed the ship and we were sinking. No one told us anything. I found out later that a fire in the engine room created a lot of smoke and confusion. No Viet Cong was attacking the ship. It would have been nice to know that at the time. Not that we could have done much of anything without weapons. We had to wait for our rifles and other field gear, until we got assigned to a company after we landed.

Everyone was anxious to get assigned to a company and to get a weapon. (Be careful for what you wish for.) When the Marine Corps gives you a weapon, they want you to use it. Once I got assigned to a company and a platoon the clerk took a picture of you. I didn't remember them taking the picture; I was not smiling. I saw the picture about 46 years later. The Marines took everyone's picture, in case you die in Vietnam. They didn't care if you smile or not.

It was a hot day; there are no cool days in Vietnam. I was hoping that I could get a weapon today. I had to wait two or three more days until someone was going home, dead or alive to get their weapon. That was the way it was. I didn't like it then, but what else could I do? Maybe go home, but I didn't think they would let me.

While I was waiting, I went over to an area a couple of hundred feet away for some water to drink another Marine said, "Put Kool-Aid in it." Someone yelled, don't forget your Iodine tables, helps kill the germs and anything else in the water. The water was warm, never cold and tasted like shit. The Kool-Aid hides the taste and the looks of the water. I used Kool-Aid, a different flavor or whatever I had, every day until I left Vietnam and never had it again. It served the purpose at that time. It camouflaged the looks and the taste of the water and it made it easier to drink sometimes. One day the company that I got assigned to ran out of water and I didn't have any for a couple of days. I was on a search and destroy mission at the time. I saw a mud hole with stagnate water in it and filled my canteen with that water. I put a handful of purification tablets in it, shook it up and drank it all. I didn't wait two hours for the pills to take effect. More like two minutes. I didn't give a shit about what could happen to me, I wanted water.

The company clerk shouted "Jerry go get your gear from the supply Sergeant." There were no phones in the jungle and there was a lot of yelling. I walked the short distance to an area that had all of our field equipment in it and was handed a rifle and my 782 gear. 782 gears consist of a pack with field equipment in it. I said, "Thanks, all this just for me?" The Marine who dropped it off was going home today, alive, thank God. Now I felt like a Marine again. At least now I had a rifle in my hands to shoot, and kill anyone that shot at me, or was in front of us while on patrol, or out in front of our perimeter. I waited for an hour for a jeep to take me up to the hill top where Kilo Company, Third Battalion, Seventh Marines, Third Platoon, called home for now.

When I got up to the lines, I was spotted as a fucking new guy (FNG) right away. It must have been my clothes and the somewhat shine that was still on the boots. I met the Company Captain, and a Lt. who told me to keep my head down. The squad leader came over to say hello and to assign me to a fire team. I don't remember any of their names. Everyone I met said, "Keep your head down. Don't do anything stupid. Watch the guys who have been here for a while and listen to them. If you are lucky, you may get to go home in thirteen months." I said, "Can I go now?" Everyone started to laugh.

They said, "Don't be a fucking pussy, bullets can only kill you and you are a Marine." They knew I was scared because of the way I looked.

They showed me an area on the lines, around the perimeter, for our company and told me to dig a foxhole as deep as I could. The deeper the better and hope that you don't get a mortar round on top of you. After you dig your hole, you will be on watch for three hours. Anything that you see in front of you, shoot to kill. Now I was shaking even more. What the fuck have I gotten into? There were other Marines around me but they were a few yards away on the perimeter. I wanted everyone around me to stop the bullets if they came in my direction. They all said, "go fuck yourself" and start digging. The hole had to be done before dark.

The first night on watch had me shaking for hours. Sweat pouring into my eyes and my hands were wet. The other Marines were only a few hundred feet away but they might as well be miles away. If someone attacked our position, it would be over for me before I got help. I was with another Marine, but it was his turn to sleep. I heard movement out in front of my position, sounds of walking or running I didn't know. I wasn't going to wake the other Marine up. I didn't want to be called a pussy, so I waited to see if I could see anything. It was dark out; there were no reflections from any light because there was none around. I heard the noise

Jerry Byrne

TUESDAY, NOVEMBER 22, 1966

MOM HAS TWIN PROBLEM

★ ★ ★   ★ ★ ★

Both Sons Are Fighting in Viet Nam

The letter from Chu Lai in South Viet Nam said casually, "We had a little get-to-gether."

Reading between the lines, Mrs. Dorothy Byrne of Howard Beach could tell that the reunion of her twin sons, John and Jerry, must have been more than just a get-together.

The husky duo—they'll be 21 the 10th of next month — had been together all their lives, even through their first two years as Marines.

But last March, Jerry was reassigned to combat duty in Viet Nam. John wasn't shipped there until June.

* * *

UNTIL that split, they'd been side by side through grammar school, Thomas Edison High School in Jamaica, boot camp in the Marines, sea duty with the fleet in the Mediterranean and at the Guantanamo Naval base in Cuba.

"The boys didn't say much in their letter," their mother said in her home at 156-13 102nd Street. "They're kidding me about bringing home a pair of wives from Viet Nam.

"I'm going to write and remind them that there are plenty of girls here."

Mrs. Byrne knew that her son, Jerry, had been assigned as an instructor to work with South Vietnamese troops in Chu Lai after he had been on combat patrols for about six months.

The other twin, John, was with an air wing in Da Nang until he was lucky enough to be reassigned to Chu Lai as a security guard last week.

The reunion shouldn't last too much longer. Under a new law, brothers aren't supposed to be in combat in Viet Nam at the same time.

The twins agreed that Jerry, who has been there longer, should be the one to leave the fighting area.

When the slow process of handling paperwork that stretches all the way to Washington is finished, the twins will be separated again.

* * *

HAVING SONS in Viet Nam combat areas is noth-

JOHN BYRNE   JERRY BYRNE

ing new for the Howard Beach mother. An older son, Dennis, was wounded by shrapnel in combat there last year. He's discharged and home now in good shape.

"I'm glad they'll have a chance to see each other on weekends now for a while," Mrs. Byrne said. "That means they'll be together for Christmas if Jerry's still there.

"Maybe next year we'll all be at home together."

Newspaper Article
Long Island Press
Tuesday, November 22, 1966

Waiting for our milk.

Couldn't wait to explore the world.

With my brothers John, Dennis & David.

Can you pick
which one is Jerry?

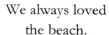

We always loved
the beach.

John & Jerry, High School Graduation - June 1963.

Jerry, Dennis and John - June, 1964.

JERRY BYRNE

1963

JOHN BYRNE

1963

Chu Lai, Vietnam - 1966.

In the jungles
of Vietnam.

On a mountaintop
in Chu Lai.

JOHN WAYNE - United Service Organization (USO), 1966.

Kilo Company 3/7 Command.

Waiting for the command to move out.

Our base command for the Combined Action
Company – 1966.

Securing the area, outside our camp.

Sleeping Area.

The well and shower area.

Jackie said, "Take a picture of this" as he lifted the only bag he picked up. Then he wrote home, "I had to fill up all these bags myself".

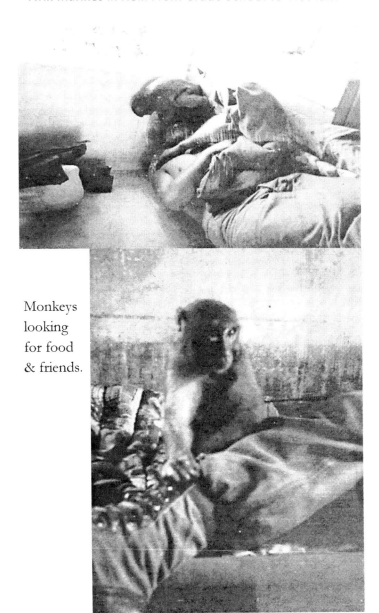

Monkeys looking for food & friends.

One of the many areas the Marines and the Popular Forces would patrol. They would set up ambushes at night.

Jerry and Jackie Byrne at my base, Chu Lai – 1966.

Jerry Byrne - CAP Camp.

Grenades on the Christmas tree wrapped in foil.

Jack Byrne - Village outside Mag 36, Chu Lai, Vietnam.

j

Captain in charge of the
Popular Forces.

Jackie and Jerry Byrne inside my command post.

I am enjoying a long walk
and a cold beer after leaving
Vietnam, but not yet home.

This was the only welcome home I received
when I returned home from Vietnam in 1967.

again and was going to shoot toward it, but waited. Scared? Damn right I was.

This was my first time in a jungle where people wanted to kill me. There were a million things going through my head on what to do if someone attacks my position. All my senses are now on full alert. I held my breath quite a few times while looking in every direction, hoping that I didn't see anyone. I could do without any action tonight or any other night. When the other Marine woke up for his watch, he wanted to know if I heard anything and I told him there was something out there. I pointed in the direction of the noise and just at that moment, a fucking monkey ran in front of us and I opened up with about twenty bullets, a full magazine. It woke up everyone on the line. I didn't piss in my pants, but it was close. The other guys never let me live that down. I slept with my finger on the trigger of my rifle almost every night after that. No matter who you are, or how long you had been in Vietnam, there are some things you can't get used to. Being up on a hill in the middle of nowhere, thinking that someone is coming to kill you in the middle of the night is just one of those things.

It will be a long 13 Months. I did pray every day that I didn't get shot, or shot at. As it turned out I was lucky, I got shot at but they missed. Half of my prayers were answered. I made it home with no physical problems that anyone could see. Mentally, I'm still not sure.

CHAPTER 11

THE DAY THE BULLETS HIT

The day started just like it did every day since I arrived in Vietnam: hot and hotter. I got to Vietnam, the first week of March 1966. They told us on ship that it was a police action; not much going on except for the heat, rain, bugs and more bugs. Police action so we were told many times. They forgot to tell us about the guys in our platoon that were killed, or wounded while taking a walk in the sunshine.

On March 20, 1966, the platoon sergeant said I was walking point, which is walking about two hundred yards or more in front of the formation of a company of Marines while we were on patrol. We were in a position of spotting the enemy first so a warning can be given to the main body of troops to our rear. But I think we were bait to entice the enemy, to shoot at us. I was with a corporal who was in Vietnam now for eight months. He knew what it was like to be in combat and to be shot at. He had some of his friends killed only a month before by the Viet Cong, when they were overrun on their hill-top position.

I had turned twenty years old in December 1965. I trained for combat for more than two years in the Marine Corps, in different countries and at Camp Lejeune, North Carolina, before getting my orders to go to Vietnam, where I was assigned to Kilo Company, third platoon, 3RD Battalion, 7TH Marine Regiment. There was no training that I could have done that would have prepared me for what was going to happen to us next.

I was walking near a rice paddy on a path, which was actually in and out of a cemetery. At least we didn't have to chop our way through elephant grass, using a machete until our arms felt like they were falling off. The enemy didn't attack in cemeteries because they were afraid of evil spirits. That's what everyone told us. It was a sunny day, and I was enjoying the fresh air and solitude around me. (If anyone can have solitude, when there are a couple of hundred Marines, with rifles, walking about three hundred yards in back of you.) I was told to watch for any movement around me, shoot and kill anything that I saw and that we don't step on any landmines or punji sticks, like we wouldn't be looking for booby traps. No one would want to step on a landmine or Punji sticks. (Punji sticks were sharpened pieces of bamboo, with poisons on the tips, which will go through the bottom of your foot if stepped on, and they were mostly buried underground.) One out of ten American casualties in Vietnam were caused by booby traps.

Being a "Fucking New Guy" and believing what I was told, I didn't really think that anyone would have the balls to shoot at this many Marines.

After being on patrol for an hour, the ground around me as I was walking, started to look like it was popping up in front of me. It started to look like small anthills, jumping out of the ground at me. There were quite a few of them. I didn't know what they were. Strange looking mounts of dirt all around me. What the fuck is this? I grew up in a partial farmland area in Howard Beach, Queens, New York. I lived far from a jungle, with weird dirt mounds. I didn't like the jungle then, and I don't like it now. It was a good thing the Marine next to me knew what it was. It turned out to be the start of a nightmare that had lasted many years for me. These were rounds from a 50-caliber machine gun, bullets hitting the ground in front and to the left and right of me. The corporal grabbed me and pushed me down, behind a tombstone. I never had anyone shooting at me before so I didn't know what was going on. Two weeks into my tour of duty in Vietnam and now I was behind a tombstone, being attacked, in an enemy cemetery, despite the spirits. I tried hard to squeeze my large body, rifle and pack behind a small tombstone. It didn't work. I didn't want to die here and get eaten by bugs. No one back home would know where I was. I would be MIA, (missing in action) lost forever, in a jungle, which I hated. Why I didn't get hit with all those bullets? I still think about that today. Didn't know why then and don't know why now. The High and Mighty was looking down on me that day and for the rest of my tour in that country.

I was scared and was not sure what to do. I couldn't see anyone in front of me but I knew that they were there because they were shooting at us. I was confused.

I was thinking that I would never see New York again or enjoy the meals that my mother used to make for my brothers and me. We were shooting back toward the machine gunner that I couldn't see but his rounds kept coming at us. I didn't know at the time how many Viet Cong were out there shooting at us. I did know that I was trapped behind a small tombstone, and couldn't stay there. I was sweating more than usual, and was wondering what the fuck would we do next? Combat was not like the old war movies where after being shot you got up and walked to the coffee wagon for something to eat.

The corporal said, "Get up and run your ass off. Run-toward the rest of the company to our rear and do it now." I said, "Yeah right, and get a hundred rounds into my back. I don't think so." He said, "Get your fucking ass moving and I will cover you." When you are running toward the rear, make sure that you're yelling: Marine coming in and hit the ground every few feet, roll your body to the left then right. As soon as you're back there, I'll start running and you will cover for me. If we don't do this now we both die. So get your fucking ass running. "Move it now!"

I ran my ass off, just like John Wayne in the movies. I think that I broke all records that day in running. Unlike in the movies, the 50-caliber bullets, going over my head and to the sides of me were real. If one 50-caliber bullet hits you in the arm or leg, you will lose that arm or leg. I was thinking that I would get many bullets into my back as I was running. I screamed many times, that a Marine was coming in, as I fell to the ground and rolled left and right every few feet. I was hoping that the other Marines didn't kill me thinking that I was the Viet Cong, attacking their position. My heart felt like it would come out of my chest; sweat poured out of me, like someone just dumped a gallon of water on me. I didn't start shaking until later and shake I did. Stress levels were just as high after a battle, because your mind has time to think about what could have happened to you.

After I ran from the tombstone and dived into a gully, a few hundred yards away, I started to shoot back toward the Viet Cong, as the other Marine came diving in next to me. He was also yelling Marine coming in. He got the Silver Star for his actions that day and the next. Our company was pinned down by enemy fire. I didn't know at that time how many Viet Cong were out there. As it turned out, there were two North Vietnamese Regiments in front of us. That's a lot of people with guns, shooting at you. About 1500 soldiers give or take. Each Regiment consisted of two battalions and each battalion had about five hundred men. There was always a shortage of troops and combat companies on both sides; they never had their full capacity of men.

There were many bullets and screams around me for the rest of the day. When Marines near you get shot, or lose an arm or leg from landmines or mortars, you never forget the sound of the pain that exits their mouths. It took a while for things to quiet down. After a few air strikes, which the commanding officer called in on the enemies' positions, the shooting quit for a short time. When you see planes flying down and dropping Napalm (a highly inflammable jelly-like substance) or bombs, a short distance in front of your position, you're happy that everyone in the village or countryside in the surrounding area and especially those who are shooting at you will be killed. There are many books written about the good and bad of bombs and napalm, but if that is what will save you from dying, so be it.

There are no tears that are going to be shed by us towards the people in the village. The Marines are going to walk away to fight another day. We were still shooting at the Viet Cong hours later.

I helped carry one of the Marines, from our platoon, covered in a poncho that died that day. Carried him until the next day to a position where a helicopter could land, and take our dead and wounded, back to the Command Post. Every time I looked at the Marine, wrapped in the poncho, I thanked God it was not me.

This was "Operation Texas," 99 Marines from my Battalion died, and hundreds were wounded. It lasted for five days from March 20th to March 25, 1966.

Welcome to Vietnam. I had twelve more months left to fight in hell. This was my first action packed operation but not my last. While in Vietnam I went on a few operations but none of them were as bad as the first. At least now if someone were shooting at me, I would know it, and could hope that their aim was not straight. Was I getting used to the shooting and being shot at? I hope not.

This was a long time ago. I put the shooting and killing, deep back into my mind as soon as I left Vietnam, hopefully to be forgotten. The names of the Marines that were killed in my platoon and the Marine that I carried for a couple of days were forgotten for many years. Last year I found out whom that Marine was and where he was from. I went to The Wall, in Washington, DC, and with tears in my eyes said, "Thank you Marine, you gave it all."

Jerry Byrne

Many of the others that were in my platoon in Vietnam died from Agent Orange, cancer or heart attacks, since 1966. The battle is still going on. There are 18 illnesses, and many forms of cancers that Agent Orange is responsible for.

My twin brother John was one of the fallen ones that died from a chemical that was made in the United States, by the Dow and Monsanto Corporations.

This chemical that the government said had no side effects on our body. The tears still flow when I think of the days before and after the war, talking to Jackie about what life had planned for us. This is one of the many reasons I go to the reunions with my Marine brothers, who were in combat with me. Tomorrow they may not be here. I need them as much as they need me to help fill in the blank spaces that I pushed to the side and deep into my mind for many years.

CHAPTER 12

THE AMBUSH

Marines getting ready to kill, that is what an ambush is about, one soldier, getting ready to kill another soldier. This soldier may or may not have volunteered to fight a war he did not want to be in. I don't think that there were many Marines, but there are always some, that looked forward to going into the jungles of Vietnam at night to wait for the Viet Cong or any enemy to cross their paths. I personally would like to be a distance away, when I shoot at the enemy. The chance of a returned bullet coming back at me would be less. I don't want to be a target.

The tension is high and I was nervous. Like a virgin hoping not to bleed, this would have been my first time on an ambush. Looking for an ambush site your whole body is on full alert. Your eyes can see all movement around you, even the grass blowing in the wind. Your body is full of energy and you feel great. Aches or pains from your body are hidden in the back of your mind, along with the fact that you are scared shit for being out there. Ten Marines walking twenty yards apart, with weapons unlocked and ready to kill, are moving on and off a small path in the middle of a jungle at night. Half of us will go to the left, with the other half going straight, looking for a good location to hide and wait for the enemy. I was loaded up with extra ammo and grenades to toss at the enemy. Every pocket of my uniform had extra ammo in it. Total weight that I had to carry was around sixty pounds. It was always better to have more ammo than less. It is not fun to be on the losing side of the ambush, because there is only one outcome for the loser: death.

Our team walked about two miles, found a good position and waited. My heart felt like it would come out of my chest and I thought that everyone could hear it pounding. I hoped that it doesn't explode in my chest in the middle of the jungle. I was smoking two or three packs of cigarettes a day and wanted a smoke. Never light up at night. We all knew the old saying; three on a match, the third guy usually gets a bullet in the head. Light can be seen for thousands of yards in the jungle at night. After an hour or so, we got up from our positions, turned around, and went back to the base camp. We did not want to let the enemy know, (if they were near us,) which group would be staying out and in what direction we would be in. I was lucky I didn't have to be on the ambush tonight. The other team secured an area about three miles out, set up a kill zone and waited. After a few hours, the enemy did walk into the kill zone. All hell broke out. The team shot and killed some of the Viet Cong and came back with one prisoner. A couple of Marines came over and hit the prisoner with the butt of their rifle. More than a few teeth came out. They wanted information on where the rest of the Viet Cong were, and didn't take no for an answer. The dead stayed where they landed. It was not our job to carry the enemy's dead back to our base camp with us. None of our guys were wounded or killed. Did I want to go? No. I would be happier to be home in New

York. An ambush can go either way. You kill them or they kill you. In the months to follow, I did go on more than a few ambushes. I was fortunate that I never got hurt. The bullets did come close to me. I did shoot at the enemy. In a combat zone, everyone's attitude towards the enemy is, "better them than me." In some situations, you may have time before pulling the trigger. Those who hesitate are lost. I would rather shed tears for the enemy than have my family shed tears for me.

The only thing that counts in a war is that you come home. The lesson we learned from war is that, "We are not fighting our friends." It is not easy to win a war on friendship.

The next morning, the platoon got together for another search and destroy mission. It seems like we are always on a search and destroy mission. We stayed on this hill a day or two, and then went on another mission, always looking for the Viet Cong. They are hiding from us. We want to kill them, before they kill us. If we got shot at, as we entered a village, or any area, we would burn down that village. That would always bring the Vietnamese's people on our side, maybe? But after burning down their homes, I didn't think so.

One day, as we got near the village, bullets started to go over my head and as long as they don't connect with me, I am happy. I shot about 60 rounds into the area in front of me. I didn't care if anyone got shot, but if they were shooting at me, they could get shot. We would check later on any hits after the village was secured. I did not care who was in the way of my bullets, as long as it was not an

117

American. After a village, was burnt down and many were, I would wonder where the people who lived there would go to live. They would probably go to the enemies' camp, they were not allowed in ours, or maybe go underground. Underground cities are common in Vietnam, and they went on for miles. We didn't know enough about them at that time. We knew there were tunnels, but didn't think they went on for miles. In some locations, there were hospitals, with hundreds of beds underground. (I now know them as the Tunnels of Chu Chi)

A Marine had to be lucky sometimes to survive. Sometimes the water and food are poisoned by the Viet Cong, with the hope that some hungry Marine wanted to eat something. (Food that could be poisoned in the area was apples, bananas, coconuts, and rice.) As we waited in our positions to move out one day, I chopped down a banana tree that was in front of me with my bayonet. I ate a couple of the bananas but I didn't die. We got the order to move out. We were told that we were going to help the ARVN'S, (South Vietnam Army) to help secure an area that the North Vietnamese took from them the day before. As it turned out, the South Vietnamese Army was of no use to us and the Americans had to secure the area themselves. After many shots were fired, we gave the village back to the people and the South Vietnamese Army hoping that they would keep it secured. I couldn't believe what I was seeing coming into the village. Our company secured the area and we had our guys, on the perimeter, to watch for any military action from the Viet Cong. The soldiers from the South Vietnamese Army were laughing and having a great time, not even concerned about keeping anyone on watch. They had cows, pigs and chickens with them, like they were going to have a fucking party, maybe a BBQ. I said, "What the fuck is this?" They don't give a shit, so fuck them. This was a common thing for the South Vietnamese Army. Kilo Co. 3/7 left the area, for another search and destroy mission. That night the village was overrun by enemy forces and half the people were killed. We didn't go back and why should we? This was no different from any other battle in Vietnam. We secured an area or hill, left after a day or two, and then came back to do it again. We all made mistakes in the jungle. Hopefully, we get to live and to talk about them. It seems like the South Vietnamese never learn and they were at war for years.

The only good thing about war is when it is over.

CHAPTER 13

SEARCH AND DESTROY

Normally, groups form a search party to help save people in disaster areas when they are in trouble. In the Marine Corps, we call it a search and destroy mission. Every day our job was to hunt the enemy, no matter where it takes us and to destroy them. The enemies were Viet Cong soldiers that needed to be killed by us.

Are we mercenaries, being paid for the number of kills that each of us wanted? "I don't think so."

If one shot is fired on us as we patrolled an area, we usually assume the whole area is hostile and would wipe out a village by burning it to the ground.

Many times, we were told that helicopters were coming to pick us up and to secure a landing zone. Tension is high within the ranks of the Marines who are ready to shoot and kill anything that moves near our landing zone. The local villagers aren't told that we would be in an area and their ignorance shows on their faces. We don't know who the enemy is. It could or couldn't be the villagers. We have to assume that everyone in our path is the enemy.

We have come to take out the enemy but mistakes are made. It is better for us if we shoot first so we are not the ones going home in body bags. No one wants to be shipped home in a black plastic bag. This type of action usually takes place a few times a month and the tensions are always high. Sometimes only a platoon is involved and not the whole company.

The worst time to be on a patrol is during the monsoon season. The rain is coming down so hard that you can't see but a short distance in front of you. Your uniform and boots are soaked, but there is nothing that you can do about it. Some of us would like to be in a tent in upstate New York, fishing or sleeping but that is not going to happen for us today. The third platoon of Kilo Company was told to go out into the jungle, check the area and get the job done.

Going into any area, we would sometimes see an old can or a cardboard box in the middle of a path or road. A Marine learns in a very short time while in Vietnam not to kick a can or anything else as you walk by. Many Marines because of a desire to kick something have lost their legs or life due to a booby trap. Forty-five years after the war, if there were a can in front of me on the beach, or any other path, I would walk by it. A hidden grenade could still be waiting for me.

CHAPTER 14

THE BUGS WILL GET YOU

This is Viet Nam 1966. Today the company commander, a Captain who was in country for six months, told us that we will be going on a search and destroy mission that will last for three or four days. (That consisted of a group of us going into the jungle looking for the enemy.) We would start out with one village near our position and then go to the next one. This would involve checking each hut and gathering all the people to check their papers. We would walk all day. Don't know how many miles we walked but it was always a long hot walk. It turned out after the first day the order changed and that we needed to secure a landing zone. We had to go into the deep jungle and walk at night to some location miles away. At night, we were hoping that the Viet Cong wouldn't see us. I think that we all made too much noise when we had to go into the rivers or jungle. I felt that it would be better for only a few guys to go on a mission, less noise better control. The only problem with that is the more guys you had in a group the more secure you may be. If only we learned to walk without making any noise.

We had to go into rice paddies many times where the water would be up to our waist. As I was walking in the water, I could feel the leeches crawling all over my body. As I continued walking, I was hoping that they didn't crawl into my ass, or on my penis or inside my penis. It is bad enough that they have to be burned off where we could see them, I don't even like to think of what would happen if the bugs are in a spot that required cutting into the body or being medevac'd out. A medevac would require Helicopters to land near us and take the Marines that are wounded or dead back to the command area to be treated, or their bodies shipped back home. At this time, a helicopter landing would give away our position.

I hope that the bugs don't go where I don't want them to go. I was lucky for the number of times I went into the water that they didn't crawl into any spots that I couldn't see. Even though many of us either tucked our trousers into the top of our boots or used a blousing strap around the boots to keep the unwanted leeches out, the unwanted can still find their way to your skin. Leeches are like rats. They can squeeze through anything. I could not deal with the pain if they did get inside me. Forty years later, I spoke to some veterans about this experience. One guy told me that leeches got into the head of the penis of a Marine in his platoon. The bayonet had to come out. There is no reason to go into the details on that. It did not go well. The Vietnam War Veterans Association or the Vietnam Veterans of America are just two of the groups that I shared my experience that I had with bugs in Vietnam.

Snakes didn't give me any problems. I only saw a handful of them. One snake was called the two-step. If it bit you, you would be almost dead in two steps. Snakes also liked to crawl into your body parts. At night, we always slept with our boots on and hoped for the best. Thank God I didn't have as many problems as other guys had.

Leeches, ticks and red ants seem to be indigenous to the area we were in. They are everywhere. But then again, anywhere that has a warm or hot climate and rain nonstop at times for weeks will also have bugs.

Living with the mosquitos 24 hours a day, many of them eating at your hands, face, neck and ears nonstop every day are enough to drive you crazy. Any chance a Marine had to pour a bottle of a liquid chemical that the military called Bug Juice on every exposed part of your body they did it. (Bug Juice would be like using "OFF" bug spray all day.) Night is the worst time because you would want to slap at these fucking bugs crawling all over you. But if you did that, it would make noise and your position would not remain hidden. So, the bugs would crawl and eat.

We would walk for hours at night and then try to get some sleep just before daybreak. We would dig into our positions and rest while the sun was out.

While walking through the jungle, our hands and face would always get cut by the tall elephant grass and bamboo. The blood would dry up most of the time but if the cut is deep, it would bleed for a while. When it was bleeding the bugs of the jungle would have a feast on your body. It seems like the bugs are calling all of their friends over to nibble on you. If you are sleeping that could be a problem.

After two nights of walking and getting our face and hands cut open by the bamboo and tall grass, the heat and pain of the jungle starts to affect the body. Your body wants to sleep but you can't do so just because you're tired. Keep pushing to get to the LZ (Landing Zone) for the helicopters to land. There will be about forty or more Marines jumping out of the helicopters and the area needs to be secured. After other Marines land, a position on top of a nearby hill would have to be secured. There is a time for us to secure the area. Only the platoon Sergeant and the First Lieutenant knew what time we had to be there, usually getting our orders a few minutes before we had to do anything. It could be a hot LZ, meaning that we could walk into enemy fire near the LZ. If we got pinned down or killed, before securing the landing zone, the Marines that are jumping out of the helicopters would surely die.

I ran out of water and my mouth was so dry that I could not talk. Some people would be happy if I didn't talk for a while and today was one of those days. We all had to be discipline with our two canteens of water. We knew that the water wouldn't last long. The decision to carry more ammo or water was with all of us. The ammo usually won. Without ammo, we could die, but without water, we would go crazy. Marines were known to be a little crazy. Maybe this was the reason.

I had to wait for more water just like everyone else, wait until the LZ was secured we were told. It was hot and sweat would pour off your body five minutes after the sun comes up. It is sometimes a little cooler at night when the sun is not burning into your skin and the need for water is as not as strong as it is in the day, but it was still needed.

I was tired and my body was full of pain. My legs, arms and hands were cut open from the elephant grass and bamboo but I was told to go forward. This isn't a picnic you are a Marine, stop acting like a pussy and keep pushing forward. We walked for hours into the jungle and finally arrived at the landing zone a few hours before sunrise. Keep down and wait for the order to be given to move out. We all took turns sleeping or closing our eyes for a while. We couldn't see around us because of the darkness but who cares, we were resting and not getting shot at.

The sun was rising and I heard the sounds of helicopters in the distance. I slept for an hour. When I opened my eyes, I realized that I was covered with red ants. I was resting on an anthill and fell asleep. I didn't want to scream out, and started to wipe them off, by the handful, from my arms and hands. They were on my face and biting my nose and ears. They were digging into the flesh and into the open wounds on my hands. This was a nightmare, I couldn't feel them biting into me. My hands were infected and puss was in every cut on my hands and face. The red ants were crawling all over my body. I wanted to strip off all my clothes and get rid of them. But you can't take off your clothes in a landing Zone and stand up if someone is out there waiting to shoot at you.

I was lucky that the LZ was not hot and we didn't have any contact with the Viet Cong. (A hot landing zone is when the enemy is shooting at you.) Once the helicopters dropped off the other Marines, we were told to move on to a different position a mile away. I quickly took off my clothes and got rid of most of the fucking ants. I was told to get my squad together, check out a hill, and secure it. I told the Captain that I couldn't open or close my hands, because of the infection. He said, "I don't give a fuck, get your ass up there with your squad and secure that hill." It was at that time I realized that this is a bullshit war. No one knew what was going on.

There was no reason to send only one squad to the top of the hill instead of the whole platoon. Lucky for me there was no enemy fire or troops at the top of the hill waiting for us. I would not be able to hold my weapon or fire my rifle if I had to because of the infection to my hands. We walked back down and joined the rest of the company. After a few hours, we started back to the command post about six miles away. I told the Corpsman, who we called Doc about my hands. (He was not a doctor but was the platoon medic who took care of the wounded as close to a doctor's care as we could get in the field.) He took one look at my hands and said, "Shit." As soon as we get back to the command post (which had a medical group available to help the wounded) you are going to the Hospital.

I couldn't hold my rifle and had it over my shoulder.

It took us a few hours to walk back to the command base. I was hoping that they would put me on a helicopter and send me back but not today. You don't get a free ride unless the enemy shoots you. They all said, "Bugs don't count, go fuck yourself and start walking."

When I got back to the command area, I walked to the hospital and the two doctors who were outside smoking looked at my hands and said, "You are staying here." I stayed in the hospital for more than a week maybe closer to two weeks. I was given shots of penicillin, twice a day, to get the fever and infection down. After a few days, I started to feel better and tried to enjoy my stay, with good tasting food three times a day and a clean bed with no bugs in them.

Only in the jungle can a hospital be enjoyable and a place I didn't want to leave. I don't think there were any air conditioners inside at that time, but I was inside a clean building and could sleep all day if I wanted to. I don't remember what I did all day, probably made passes at the nurses. The nurses did a great job and did not always get the recognition that they deserved while being in Vietnam or when they came home. I do know being in the hospital was better than walking on patrol in the jungle and getting shot at.

Good things had to end and I went back to Kilo Company and the Third Platoon for a few more months in hell. The bugs were waiting for me. I couldn't kill all of them that found my sweet arms and neck. I guess they were all happy bugs because they liked to bite deep and eat they did. Some of them died with a smile on their face and food in their mouths.

CHAPTER 15

THE FRENCH FORT

The shadows of the night started to disappear as I looked out into the jungle of Chu Lai. I had an easy night while I was on perimeter watch up on our lines in Vietnam looking over at the mountains a distance away. I didn't see any falling stars or anything else tonight. The sun started to pop up; it is always a good night when no one is shooting at you. I did like the sunshine more than the darkness of the night. With every inch that the sun was moving above the horizon, it was getting hotter and hotter like it did every day. Just like a large crystal, rays of light were shining in every direction. Sweat would pour out of your body all day. The sweat started as soon as the sun came out. Most days it is around 100 degrees, give or take 10 degrees.

It would be nice to take a cold shower or at any temperature that the water may be. But sometimes in the field, it would be weeks before you could find a river or waterfall to get clean. Even after washing yourself and soaking your clothes to get the stink out of them, the same clothes will have to be put back on. Since the clothes are already wet with sweat, everyone tries to wash them as often as they could with soap, if we had soap. Walking in swamp water and falling in rice patties takes a toll on your mind and body and the clothes on your back. It was a wonderful pleasure when we could find a body of water to cool off in.

As I was walking down the hill to the command post, the Commanding office called me over to where he was sitting under a tree and said, "Corporal, I got a nice job for you." The Marine Corps does not give you any easy or nice jobs to do in the jungle or back on base in the United States. Since I didn't have a choice I said, "Yes Sir! I am looking forward to doing an easy job." He knows and I know that we were both bullshitting each other. "I will do a good job Sir."

The job is to take your squad, (usually 12 men) and help secure an old French Fort on the other side of that mountain. He was pointing to the mountain east of our position. This was more or less a sign of good will that a group of Marines could help the South Vietnam Army and secure a position with them. I turned to look and was hoping that we did not have to walk over there though the jungle and up the mountain.

He said, "The jeeps or trucks would be coming at 10:30 A.M. I want everyone to lock and load and to watch each other's back." He didn't have to say that because any time we were in the field there is a round in the chamber of the rifle and the safety was off. The chain of command didn't like anyone walking around with a loaded rifle. Someone should tell them that we are in a combat zone and our hands should be untied. Everyone I knew had a round in their weapon and the safety was off. At any given time someone could shoot at you and you didn't want to wait a few seconds to shoot back.

Believe it or not, the trucks were on time and we didn't have to hurry up and wait. It only took about fifteen minutes to load our equipment on to the trucks and then we were moving to the other side of the mountain. I had no fucking idea what we were going to do once we got to the ARVN Camp. (Army of the Republic of South Vietnam) I didn't trust any of them at that time in 1966 and I don't think I would trust them now. We were told that we would be there for 3 or 4 days by our Platoon Commander, a 2nd Lieutenant. I was not happy to go but I went anyway. Marines don't have a choice. I didn't know what to expect when we got there. I did know that I would decide what orders my squad will follow. Not that I knew anything more about war than anyone else but I thought that if we are being put in danger then the South Vietnamese army can go fuck themselves. Even though the country was at war for years before we got there, there were many infantry companies, within their army that didn't know what they were doing. Their attitude was that someone else would fight for them and maybe give them everything that they need.

Thank God it was not raining when we were going across and up the dirt road. It took us and hour or two to get there and no one was shooting at us. We reported to the Commanding Officer of the camp and were told where to set our packs and the rest of our 782 equipment.

It was a small building in the corner of the camp. It had a few windows, or opening, where windows should have been. It didn't take us long to settle down and secure our area. We all went outside to look around the camp and to try to communicate with the soldiers that were near us. We had our area to set up a perimeter watch at night. During the day, we were not as tense because there were about a hundred men in the camp and many people from the nearby village were allowed in. An attack during the day in this area was not likely. The people from the village would more than likely shoot at us at night after seeing our positions in the daylight. We know that is what they will try to do, and we would be ready for them. We wouldn't get into our positions until after dark. Every one of us was aware of our surroundings and was prepared to shoot to kill, if we had to. We didn't depend on others in the camp for our safety.

While outside our building or hut as some would call our living area on the second day, some of us were playing ball or trying to write a letter home or just taking it easy. We didn't get much sleep at night, so if we can get a few minutes of sleep we usually did. After a while we got used to sleeping on the ground with our head resting on our helmet and our finger always on the trigger of our rifle.

One of the Marines standing outside, near the back of the building, or hut as some would call it; saw someone going through our packs inside the building. It only took us a few seconds to surround the place and grab the guy. We were pissed that they were trying to rob us of our few belongings. Most of us had extra cigarettes and socks, which we needed along with our c-rations and packs of coffee from 1943. (C-Rations were left over food supplies, in sealed lead lined cans. Beef, pork, eggs and ham and lima beans, to name a few that were packed during WWII.) Another reason why we all lost weight around 20 to 30 pounds in Vietnam. One of our guys had the thief on the ground and already started punching him in the face. The commander of their group came over and said that they would punish the soldier themselves. We didn't believe them but because of where we were, we didn't have much choice. We were outnumbered. We had to play nice.

Some of us decided to go into the village a short distance from the front gate. The front gate is not like a gated community that you might see in a retirement area such as Florida. The front gate had two or three troops from the Vietnamese army, standing watch, within a wall of sandbags for protection. We always wanted to know if the people of Vietnam liked us or not. We are here in this country for them, so we all thought in 1966. It is hard to tell their feelings because they are always smiling when they see us. Most countries that Americans go into, the people want our money first and then whatever else we can give them. Their hands are always out. Children run toward us laughing and with smiles on their faces. Sure, we like to see that, but in our minds, we do not trust any of them and might be forced to shoot them if our lives were on the line. In Vietnam, our lives are on the line every day.

As we were walking across the road, there were 10 or 12 troops from the Vietnam army from our camp, sitting down at small tables, drinking and talking to the local girls from the village. As we got nearer to the tables on the other side of the store toward the rear from where the Vietnamese troops were sitting, one of them jumped up and pointed his rifle at me. I guess he wanted to impress his girlfriends on how tough he was against the American Marines. (Americans who are sweating their asses off and getting shot at in a country 10,000 miles from home.) I can usually let things go by me so that someone could impress his girl, but not a weapon being pointed at me. We are at war it is not a game. I punched out at his face and grabbed the rifle from him. My guys had their rifles pointed at the troops sitting down and would have opened fire if it was needed. We just got there and we were not looking to shoot the troops that we were supposed to be friends with. There were still about 100 guys on the other side of the gate. I decided that it was time to leave and go back to the base on the other side of the gate. The guys agreed with me and were ready to go. I still had the South Vietnamese rifle in my hand. I took the bullets out of the weapon and flung it across the road as far as I could, then told the guy that he was a scrum bag and pushed him. We all turned to go back to the base. I knew that this incident would create a lot of tension for us but all of my guys were happy that I did it. We didn't need bullshit. We were outnumbered, but that doesn't mean we have to put up with bullshit.

The commanding officer came over to us and said that this would not happen again and his guy was sorry. We didn't believe him, but we tried to let it go. We still would not trust them and we couldn't wait to leave this area. Maybe only a few more days here then we will be back with our own platoon. A platoon of men who can trust each other with their lives and all of us were watching each other backs.

Some of us were outside sitting around, when a few guys from the camp came over to us and wanted to test our skills at fighting. A couple of Marines stood up and got into a boxing position. The Vietnamese didn't want any part of that, looked at me, and got into a martial arts stand. A karate stand (The art of empty hand fighting.) I looked at them and said no. I was in charge and I guess the leader of this group of Marines. One guy was persistent and was circling around me throwing punches near me to show off his form. I did many hours of free style sparring and boxing, with my brother Jackie growing up in Howard Beach before joining the Marines. I didn't think I would have any problems sparring with this guy. The only problem is the attitude of the Vietnamese when they lost. There was no respect now for us and when I kick his ass it would be even less. The guy that was punching at the air said, "Marines can't fight," and all his friends were agreeing with him. No one from my group knew anything about Karate, some knew how to box a little but that wasn't the game now. The guys said, "Can you do it Jerry?" and I said yes.

I got up and took off my shirt and boots to give myself better movement. I got into an open leg stand then gave a bow. I then got into a forward stand, started to walk around the Vietnamese soldier, and threw a few punches, not connecting because this was sparring, not full contact. We were not there to hurt anyone. After a few minutes the Vietnamese jumped up and hit me in my shoulder with a flying sidekick full contact, it forced me back and I felt the pain. The game had changed and now I was pissed off. I came forward with a few front snap kicks. I was out for the kill and didn't care if the guy got hurt. I hit him across the face with four or five punches and then kicked him, as hard as I could in the chest. The kick landed him on his ass and all of his friends were, telling him to get up and fight. He did the right thing and said, "No more." No one else wanted to do any more sparring so we called it a day. It seem like I made a lot of friends that day. We got the word from the base command, after we had some C-rations for dinner that we were leaving tomorrow morning. We were only in the camp two days and I think all of us were happy to be getting out of here.

There was much concern about the watch that night. After all the shit that went on with the Vietnamese troops, we would have to be on full alert. We not only had to look for the Viet Cong in front of us, but worry about the South Vietnamese army that were in behind and around us as well. There were only 10 or 12 of us and more than a hundred of the South Vietnamese.

If it came down to a fight, I hoped that we wouldn't run out of ammo. We were all in agreement; if we take any fire from the rear of our position we should all turn around and shoot anything that moves to our rear. The enemy we knew was in front of us, our friends we hoped were to our rear. We would like everything to be peaceful and we all said a prayer that it wouldn't come down to that. As it turned out, things went well for us. We all watched the sun come over the horizon the next morning and we all felt a little more at ease. We were still looking to our front and back positions for any early morning attack, but we didn't think that was likely. The sun was hot and bright after only a few minutes and would only get hotter during the day. We all started to pack up our equipment and say our goodbyes, to the Vietnamese troops that were closer to our position. We did eat some of our C-rations, but no one ever eats all of their food at the same time because we have to save some for another day. We don't really know when we will get more supplies. That goes for the water also, water is more important. You can go without food for a few days but not water. Anyone will kill for water if they really need it.

At 11:30 that morning, the trucks were seen in the distance. By 12:30 p.m. we were ready, the trucks were loaded, and a few guys had their rifles in a guarded position, pointing to the front and rear of the truck, in case we get fired upon going back. Some of us closed our eyes going back to our camp and I fell asleep. We get our sleep whenever we can. The shit can hit the fan at any time and you would have to be up for hours. The trucks got back around 5:00 p.m. and we went right to the supplies for more water and food. It was not like we could get as much as we would like but we did eat a little more in the camp. We were happy to see the other guys from our platoon and knew that we would be more protected with an American Marine combat company.

The next morning we were told to go on a search and destroy mission, which may require setting fire to a village if we had any hostile fire toward us. The day started for us waiting for the helicopters to land and the choppers flying off with us into the jungle to look for the enemy.

We did get fired upon, but the helicopters landed anyway and we all jumped off as quickly as possible. You would be surprised at how fast someone could run when being shot at. Some of us jumped off the helicopter before it landed, about four or five feet from the ground. We are an open target any time we are in the air. After an hour of walking, we got to a location and were told that there was a possibility of Viet Cong in the village directly in front of us. My squad was on the south side of the village, ready to open up, and let the bullets fly into the village if necessary. We did hear a few rounds going off but didn't know if we should open up or not. We were told to stay down and settle in for the night, set up a watch, and be ready to move out if we got the word.

"Does anyone know what we are doing in this fucking country?" We go to one place and stay for a few days, leave and then come back three weeks later. No wonder after a few weeks in this shit hole we want to burn everything down. I was behind a banana tree and decided to cut it down, which I seem to do often. I didn't care what anyone said and the tree came down. The next morning when they told us we were leaving, I took a small candle out of my pack and placed it on top of some straw. I was hoping that the straw would catch on fire and the village will burn down to the ground after we left. I did see smoke coming from the village a few minutes after we left, maybe other guys also had the same idea. I didn't see any reason to keep coming back to these places every few weeks. I would have liked to see "Puff the Magic Dragon" come in, shoot up the whole area and kill everyone in the village. Puff the Magic Dragon was an AC-47 gunship that could shoot 18,000 rounds into a target area in a minute. I wished that we used this type of firepower more often to get the job done.

It was time for our platoon to move out and continue our search and destroy mission to places unknown. It would be a few days before we got back to our main camp.

CHAPTER 16

THE VILLAGE

The day seemed like it would be a little cooler than in the past few weeks but it was still hot. I was on top of a hill looking out into the surrounding jungle, on watch since two in the morning. It was now five and the sun was peeking out of the clouds and it brightness was shining directly at me. The many shadows from the night were now gone. It did rain last night and I was still wet. In ten minutes, I would be dry from the sun. Then my clothes would be wet again, a few minutes after that, but this time with sweat. You would think that we would all smell, and maybe we did. But we didn't know it. I guess we all smelled the same. There were times we would go for weeks without having a chance to get washed. "Don't we all just love this place?" That is why so many guys like the song by the Animals, from 1965, one of the greatest songs of all time. "I want to get out of this place, if it is the last thing I ever do" This song was immensely popular with anyone that was in Vietnam. The louder you sang it, the better it sounded (Maybe it will come true.)

The platoon was just on a search and destroy mission for a week and it felt good to be in one spot for a while, instead of running and walking in elephant grass and rice patties all day and night. Being in one spot had its downfall also, we could be attacked or have mortars dropped on us.

I started to walk down the hill toward the Command Post and saw that they had some hot food and coffee for us. This was brought in from the main base a few miles away. This was one of the pleasures that we can dream about, but it didn't happen that often. There were a few guys drinking coffee and talking about what they had heard recently. Marine Corps were looking for volunteers to work with the Popular Forces in a village, a distance from where we were. There will be 12 to 15 Marines in a camp and those Marines would decide what to do about patrols and ambushes with the local forces. This will be a Combined Action Company (CAC, 1965) the name was later changed to CAP (Combined Action Platoon). This was something new that the Marines just started doing throughout Vietnam. Working with people from a village, who for whatever reason didn't join their own military. Many of these people don't like the United States, and had many different reasons not to like us, but they always wanted our money and sometimes our help. The Marines would set up security and defend the area from the Viet Cong. It would also be an extension of our combat force near our base, an Air Field that will also give the Air Force personnel extra security.

No one would want a bullet in the back from people, (Popular Forces) who tell Americans that everyone that is in front of their foxholes or while on patrol near the river is a friend or cousin. There would only be 12 to 15 Marines in that group, by themselves in the middle of a village. Who would volunteer to join that group? Not me.

The guys around me said, "This was crazy, it can't be for real," Everyone said that they wouldn't volunteer to go out on patrol or an ambush with people who you couldn't trust.

This was the next to the last day in July 1966. I was enjoying a hot cup of coffee, and some powered eggs. I know that doesn't sound appetizing, but after C-Rations, powered eggs would be like a gourmet meal. We were still talking about how crazy it would be to go on patrol with the Popular Forces. The First Lieutenant came over to us and said, "Good morning guys." He said, "How are you doing Byrne" and I looked at him and said, "Ok, Sir." Why did he call my name out?

He said, "I got some good news for you corporal, what you volunteered for just came in this morning and you will be on the first helicopter that lands over there, this morning." Pointing at an open area, a thousand feet away from where we were sitting. "You will be going to the Chu Lai Defense Command, outside Chu Lai in a small camp with 15 other Marines that also volunteered."

My mouth dropped open and I said, "This was a mistake Sir. I would not have volunteered for this."

He said, "That is alright Marine; we did it for you, no need to thank us. We want to make life easier for you. You are needed in a new location."

All I could say was, "Yes Sir (under my breath, I said scumbag) lieutenant." Why was I going? Not for my leadership ability, that's for sure. I didn't have any problems with anyone in the platoon and I think that I held my own in the field. I may have gotten excited a few times and wanted to shoot someone, but that was normal for the locations we were at. I found out afterwards that they just pulled a name out of the hat, and said he is going. It would only take me ten minutes to go back up the hill and get my things together.

The other Marines that were in the position on line with me couldn't believe I was leaving. I told them to go down and get some coffee and hot eggs, while I packed up my things. I was with Kilo Company, 3rd platoon, 3rd Battalion, 7th Marines since March 12, 1966. I said good-bye to the guys and said I would keep in touch. 46 years later, I connected back to my past life by going to a reunion for all members of Kilo, 3/7. Maybe the next reunion I will meet someone who was in my squad. I waited for 3 hours for the helicopter to come to pick me up. Hurry up and wait. That seems like that is the normal way every day in the Marine Corps. No one knew anything about going on patrol with the Vietnamese people. I can't imagine sitting all night in a foxhole on watch looking for Viet Cong and trusting these Popular Forces, with my life if the Viet Cong charged our position one night. This adventure would not be fun.

I could never understand why the United States would help train an army; who could use that training against us. We are friends today, but we could be the enemy tomorrow.

On August 1, 1966, I checked into the Headquarters of the Chu Lai Defense Command. I did keep all of my 782 gears, (Field equipment, which consists of a backpack, water canteens, e-tool and rifle) which were given to me at Kilo

Company. After a few hours, I received some new clothes and also new boots. The uniform I had on was falling apart from the heat, sweat and rain. The boots had holes in them from walking hundreds of miles in rice patties. Since I was in the rear at Battalion headquarters, I headed for the chow line. In the mess hall, I got a steak dinner with a piece of hot cherry pie with ice cream on top. First real food I had in about 6 months. I could have eaten more but was happy with what I got. I had to wait until I left Vietnam to get another meal like that. The Marines, who stayed in the rear, had it easier compared to the grunts (infantry men). The chance of getting shot at or mortars landing in your position were at a minimum on the base. There was always a company of Marines guarding the perimeter of the base. A sergeant called out and told me to be ready to leave in five minutes. I waited an hour for the jeep to take me into a village that was a few miles away.

The Village was outside of Mag 36, an Air Force Base, about a mile or so from the main gate of the base. It was on the KY Ha Peninsula. The village itself was fairly large and had a five to seven mile perimeter that needed to be patrolled and ambushes had to be set up all day and night. We were the first CAC outfit in the area (Combined Action Company.)

I was greeted by a few of the other Marines that arrived there a few hours before me. One of them was a sergeant, and he would be in charge of us. We all came from a combat outfit and were all in a few large operations and shot at while walking point or setting up ambushes. The sergeant was of Mexican descent, and could fit in with the Vietnamese people easier than the white Marines because of the color of his skin. There were two other Mexican Americans also coming to join us today. As it turned out, all three Marines learned Vietnamese fluently and in a short period of time. When I was on patrol with them, the local people thought that they came from Saigon and were Vietnamese. I don't think they ever told them that they were not Vietnamese, especially the women. The girls couldn't get enough of them and they couldn't get enough of the girls. Was I jealous at times? Yes, but I got over it.

We all looked out for each other and it was good to have someone who spoke Vietnamese on our side that we could trust.

We all got familiar with the surrounding area while waiting for the rest of the Marines to come and join us. Everyone had an input on the best way to secure the perimeter. We did take over an old building and wanted to secure that building and the area a few hundred yards in front of us in all directions. The first night we had to decide on the watch list and also who would go on patrol. We all wanted to see what was out there and how far the area was that we would be walking every night. I was with two other Marines on patrol the first night, without any of the popular forces. We didn't trust them yet and probably never will. We were not going to be walking point and have these gooks walking behind us with loaded rifles. In a few days, we would allow them to be with us on patrol, but they would be walking in front of us. No one was going to be taking any chances, even though the probabilities of getting ambushed were low at this time.

The next morning after resting a few hours, from a long night of patrols, everyone started to fill sandbags. There was always someone on watch, while the rest of us were filling sandbags or sleeping. Most of us only had a few hours of sleep each day. There were thousands of bags that we had filled. We started around the entrance of the first house, (there was two of them) because that was where we would be sleeping. We stacked about eight to ten sandbags high and sometimes six or seven foot across, in some locations, a little higher and wider. Around each window where glass used to be thirty years ago, or maybe not ever, these were just holes that needed to be secured, so sandbags went around the opening where we could shoot out if necessary. All of this took about three weeks for the camp to be secured the way we needed it.

One day while I was chopping down trees and brushes, the local people from the village watched me work up a sweat and waited. When I was finished, the scumbags who didn't even offer to help clear the area came with large carts, wheel barrels or little wagons for the firewood. The people always had their hands out for someone to help them. It was always one-sided with them. They did use the wood for cooking. (We didn't need it because all we had to eat was C-rations.) The government never wanted to waste anything but our money, so the Marines got all the left over garbage, that none of the other armed services wanted.

One day we decided to close up the windows with shutters and to pay a local village carpenter a few dollars for thick wooden windows. We needed solid windows that could close and overlap each panel tightly. We didn't want any light from the candles that we used at night shining out into the darkness. The old carpenter charged us after an hour of negotiation his best price for the job, two dollars a window and he would supply the wood and all the material for the job. They were solid oak wooden windows that were an inch thick. It may not always stop bullets, but it did help somewhat by making us feel secure inside our compound. If that were done in America, even back in the 60's, it would have cost about a hundred dollars a window. All the Marines contributed one or two dollars each. We had to pay for it because the government told us to sleep in tents. The carpenter didn't even make near that much money for the year from other sources. He may also come back some night to try and kill us, (friends in the day, Viet Cong at night.) We didn't need any light shining out into the darkness through the windows. The carpenter may have been a Viet Cong sympathizer for all we knew and we didn't want to give anyone the opportunity to put a bullet in our head from a sniper round. We never knew whom to trust, so we never really trusted any of them. What a way to live, always looking over your shoulder.

Every three or four nights I would be on a patrol or go out and set up an ambush. Other nights I guarded our perimeter. I would take two guys from the Popular Forces with me and every night that we go out it would be the same outcome. They would say that there is no VC (Viet Cong) out here or if we did come across anyone, it would be a cousin or friend of theirs. We would be about two miles from our base headquarters sitting in a hole or surrounded by rocks and brushes, waiting for any activity from the Viet Cong that may be in the area. If they walked in front of us we would open up and hopefully kill a few of them. Most nights it was quiet but I would never sleep and let the PF'S keep watch. I would get a couple of hours of sleep, when I got back to the camp where I knew that my fellow Marines were on watch.

Your mind gets worn down on watch all night and after a while, every tree has arms and legs and there are times you want to open fire and shoot anything that could be out there but you wait to see if there is any real movement. Tension is always at its peak and the urge is to open fire with everything you've got. It is important not to give away your position. The Viet Cong knew that Americans are out there but they don't know how many or where the location would be. Every night we would pick a different place.

One night I felt like John Wayne and was patrolling near the riverbed. I was for some unknown reason by myself. There were only two or three stupid moments that I was not with other Marines. There are always some stupid things that are done in combat, this was one of them. Lucky for me I lived to talk about it. I saw a sampan, a small circular boat that was used by the Viet Cong and many local farmers throughout South Vietnam with one person in it. It was one of those days that I felt that I was in charge and these South Vietnamese people will listen to me.

I was standing next to a thin tree as I called the person on the sampan to come in. I was also pissed off that we are not doing all we could do to win this war, so I shot a few rounds over the head of the person in the sampan. He didn't like that. He fired the machine gun that he had hidden with him right at me. That scared the shit out of me and I dropped to the ground and shot about 60 rounds back at him. I was hoping to kill him, but he moved quickly away from the shoreline. I guess I am a bad shot. You can't win them all. I did call in my position, and the command sent a few mortars into the water a few hundred feet from where I was hiding. In a few minutes, four Marines from the camp were running over to help. They all told me that I was a fucking ass for going on my own. They were right.

We are in Vietnam to gain the confidence of the villages and to try to stop the Viet Cong from coming in. I guess I did my part? I always thought afterward that I should have just waved to the guy and continued on my patrol. I always said expect the unexpected, I should have listened to myself. But it turned out to be a good night. They missed me.

Every time I was out on patrol after that, I made sure that I was walking between bigger trees and other Marines were with me.

We did such a great job of fixing the buildings that we were using, that one day the Village chief or Mayor (every leader used a different title that the people would call him) came into the campsite and said he wanted the building back. I wanted to shoot him and told him to go fuck himself. We are in Vietnam to help these people not to be taken advantage of. It was up to the Sergeant in charge of us to deal with him. We made this place look like a palace compared to the grass huts and broken down structures that was surrounding us for miles; we were not going to give it up. The sergeant made it clear to the village leader and to all of us that we are here to help them but not to give up our campsite, a site that was falling apart for forty years before we got to Vietnam. We needed this site to protect the rest of the people in the area. I think the sergeant said he would help the chief build a nice big home, down the road near the water, for free.

Everyone knows that nothing is free. The chief had a cute looking daughter that the sergeant liked, and took full advantage of that fact. The sergeant also took advantage of the daughter. Being a politician of course, the chief agreed. He told the other villages that we could stay, because we were going to help them. He became our eyes and ears, while I was there. We helped him and he helped us, but I still wouldn't trust him. I have a lot of trust issues.

One day we got word that a company of Popular Forces are going to have an inspection of their equipment inside our compound. That would be their rifles, uniforms and packs, like the Marines; they called all of this equipment the 782 gear. As it turned out, I got pissed off the minute that about 200 PF's came into our headquarters.

These are men somewhere around twenty years old. Why are they in the village and not in their army? I was twenty years old and already in the Marines for three years and being shot at in their country. "Fuck them." Their equipment was brand new and better than ours. Uniforms with no holes in them and boots that had a shine you can see from a distance. This is a war zone? I don't think any of them ever fired at the Viet Cong, or anyone else with their rifles. Maybe they may have fired at us with other weapons, than buried their rifles in the ground and walked by us, smiling and looking happy like they were our best friends.

This inspection and get together lasted about four or five hours, with the women and children coming into the area to eat. Thanks to the United States for all of the hot food and drinks. Children wanted to play and jump all over our sandbags, foxholes, and of course to see what they could steal when we were not looking. Marines came from the battalion rear area, about two or three miles from our command post with four jeeps filled with all the hot food and cold drinks, to be given only to the people in the village. I started a fight because I wanted a cold soda and a hot turkey sandwich. I did get one. We are putting our lives on the line every day for the Vietnamese people; the least that the high command can do for us is give us a treat once in a while. There were only twelve to fifteen of us guarding the village. It still pisses me off even today when I think about what happened in 1966. An hour before the darkness started to move into the base we told everyone to leave. There are always one or two people that said, no not yet. I said, "Move your fucking ass off our base." The Captain of the PF'S, heard the shouting, ran over to the two PF'S that were causing trouble. He didn't say anything to the PF'S. The Captain just started to kick and punch both of them until they were on the ground and not moving.

They said they were sorry when they got up a few minutes later. I was happy to see that at least the captain cared about his country and for the security of the village. Just another reason for the PF'S to walk in front of us on patrol. When it got dark, I went on a patrol for four hours. We all had different times to set up ambushes and patrols. Sometimes we would stay out for only an hour and then came back to the base to sleep a few hours before going out on another patrol.

There is always someone out there on patrol and someone on watch around our camp. Two or three hours of sleep a day were usually enough for most of us. Every night there was something else happening on patrol. If we saw anyone on the river, we would now shoot at them and hopefully they don't shoot back. Since we were also protecting the Air Base along with the village, every time we shot our weapons, an officer from the base would come over the next morning to ask why. They wanted to know if it was necessary. Of course, it was always necessary. It would seem that the officers or anyone from the base didn't really think we were in a combat zone. If someone started to shoot at them in the middle of the night, they would know soon enough that it was for real. The officers were so far in the rear it was like being on vacation for them.

One night as a helicopter was flying over our area to land at the Air Base a mile away, it took a few rounds from the ground. The crew opened up with their automatic weapons and shot back towards the ground. The helicopter crew did shoot down into the village; maybe they were fired upon, maybe not. They did spray the area with bullets, which was ok by me, and the rest of the Marines. The next morning a Lieutenant from headquarters was asking me, "Did you see rounds being fired, from the ground?"

"Of course I did" I said. I wanted to say, "What the fuck was wrong with you Sir? We are in a war zone Sir. There is always shooting from the ground Sir, and your candy ass, never sees it because you are watching movies or screwing some nurse. When are the politicians going to let us fight to win?" This shit went on every two or three weeks.

A few weeks after I got to the camp my brother Jackie was transferred from the Da Nang Air Base, to the Chu Lai Air Base, which is only a short distance from where I was. He got himself in trouble one day by telling an officer to get off the helicopter that was going from Chu Lai to Da Nang Air Base. His job was to drop off mail, or documents, to and from each base. He had the right to have a seat on the helicopter, but when it comes to officers, don't be a wise ass. Jackie always wanted to fuck with the officers. The three colonels stayed on but the major or captain had to leave, and Jackie told him to get off. Jackie wanted to get back to dance and drink with the nurses or girls from the U.S.O. (United Service Organization) show that were at the base. There were many hot girls who wanted to dance, and drink every day. The food was hot and the best that the air forces could serve. Who wouldn't tell the officer to get off? Jackie said, "Fuck the officer, I have the right to stay on." They even had a swimming pool that he jumped into every day and maybe at night with the nurses. Three or four weeks after this incident, he was taken from an easy position to a more demanding one. He was still inside an Air Force Base, but now he had to stand guard duty and watch for the Viet Cong trying to sneak through the perimeter.

His chance of getting hit by a sniper just increased more than 100%.

One day as I was going on a search for the enemy around the perimeter of the village, a mile outside the base, I walked right into my brother Jackie. "What the fuck are you doing here?" I asked. The village was open to the Marines from the base during the day, but they must return by 1600 hours (4:00 p.m.) He was with a couple of his friends and they wanted a few beers and to talk to some of the local girls, in broken English. They did sell American beer in the village, which the Vietnamese probably robbed from the docks, or bought on the black market. Someone was getting paid off. There were times that I wanted to just take the beer, without paying. These supplies did belong to Americans.

One day the South Korean Marines came into the village for an hour after training at the Air Force Base. They didn't pay for anything. If they were told by the merchant to pay, they would hit the merchant with the butt of their rifle and take it anyway. Was it the right thing to do? My mind is still at odds with the right or wrong when it comes to the actions of war. One day they wanted me to pay for a coconut that I got off a tree, I wanted to shoot everyone. "This is bull shit," I said. "We are here to fight for them and their fucking country." I wanted a coconut, and I was taking it. "Fuck them." Let someone else pay them if they are so concerned, I am not paying. Someone else did pay for it. Some officer who wanted to look good and never was in a combat situation took money out of his pocket and gave it to the village chief.

My brother Jackie did come into my area every time he came into the village. It was always good to see him. He knew that he could be shot at by walking around, but it was not likely during the day. The people in the village wanted the American money, so they didn't want anything or anyone interfering with the buying or selling of goods in the village. The village could be closed to base personnel if someone got shot or hurt during the day.

One day when Jack walked into my camp, he saw all of us filling sandbags. He turned around walking away said, "Call me when you are done." I will be over there, having a beer and looking for a girl, pointing to a spot in the shade, a few hundred yards outside our gate. Good thing he was my brother, I wanted to run over and punch the shit out of him. He came back the next day, picked up one sandbag, and said, "Take a picture of this." I did. He wrote home and told everyone he did all the work filling every sandbag and it wasn't even his command post.

We are identical twins and to see us together, people couldn't tell us apart. We did play tricks on many of the Marines that we were stationed with.

One day I was walking through the village and I heard a guy shout "John Byrne!"

"Wow I didn't see you in over two years John, now we are together in the middle of Vietnam. Shit, what are the chances of that? Let me buy you a beer, John, how the fuck are you, John?" As it turned out, he was buying me beers for 3 hours and then something to eat. I knew that my name isn't John and because Jackie (John) and I were so close, I could guess at what he was doing on liberty, or where ever he was stationed. I talked to this guy about where Jackie was last year, and the other Marines in our platoon. He had no reason to not believe I was John. He said he had to return to the base before it got dark, and I said, "Thanks for the beer and food." As he was walking away toward the gate, I said, "Thanks again for everything. I don't know why you keep calling me John, but my name is Jerry." He looked at me in shock, and said, "Isn't your name John Byrne?"

I said, "No, my name is Jerry." He knew that John can joke around, but he didn't know that he had a twin brother. He said, "Bull shit! You knew where we were stationed and what we were doing, how can you not be John Byrne? What is wrong with you, John? Did you flip out over here? We were just bullshitting for three hours." The guy was getting excited. I looked at him like he was going crazy and said again that my name was not John. I had to tell him the truth, after a few minutes.

I said, "I am Jack's twin brother and know who you are because Jack talked about you many times." I had to play a joke on you and said I will buy you lunch the next time our paths crossed. He still did not believe me. I had to show him a few pictures of us together.

He said, "Shit." Shaking his head he said, "Fuck you, you better buy me more than a few beers, after what you just pulled on me. I can't believe this. Wait until I tell the guys that John's brother is just like him. What do you guys do with your girl friends? Shit, I can't believe this." With that he went through the gate, and I never saw him again. John did see him a few weeks later and had to buy him a few beers and lunch. I got a good meal out of him anyway.

Living in the village was interesting at times. It was not the best set up, but we had a roof over our heads, and we did keep everything clean. We still were outside when we were on watch. Once our watch was over and we went inside to rest, it seemed to be more relaxing, somewhat more secure and not as many bugs.

One day we found a dog or the dog found us. The dog was running near our gate so we took him in and gave him a bath and something to eat. He was a happy looking dog. We didn't know it until a few days later that he was going to be someone's supper. The women, who owned the dog, came looking for him in our compound. We weren't giving the dog up. After he was clean and had something to eat, he didn't want to leave us. Americans have dogs and cats for pets, while other countries eat anything that moves. It was a good reason for the dog to stay inside our gate. I think he knew he was safe with us and I don't think he wanted to be eaten. I don't know how long the dog stayed with us, but he was still there when I got my orders to return to Okinawa, towards the end of January, 1967.

I did eat dog meat in the village one afternoon, mixed up with rice and sauce. I asked the person that was doing the cooking what happened to the dog that was always hanging around in the front of his place. He pointed at my plate and said, "You just ate him." It was a good meal.

My brother Jackie was in the village one afternoon in December, and saw a guy taken pictures for the Stars and Stripes military newspaper. I was walking down the road and Jackie called me over, said he was going to jump up and down and scream that he thought I was dead, and will start to cry.

John was going to do all of this to get our face in the military newspaper. He always had a way of saying something and you would swear that it was true. I got away with things like that sometimes, but John always got away with it. He could say something without smiling. No matter how off the wall something will sound, people would believe him. I said, "Fuck you. I don't care about shit like that." The guy with the camera walked the other way, and Jackie lost his moment for glory. I think back on that now and I should have listened to him. I think that we would have been in the books being the only twins that were together in the same area in the "Nam." We went into a small hut and had a cold beer. The Vietnamese that were connected to the United States Military base were being taken care of. They got gas operated refrigerators and got to sell cold beer and soda to American troops. It is crazy but every time we had a drink, we thought we were going to be poisoned but we would drink it anyway. Some guys were poisoned and died. Being young, we thought it would not happen to us. We were in a combat zone where many of the people didn't like us, but still wanted our money.

Jackie and I got together many times, in the few months that we were near each other. Every time he came into the village, I would worry about him. I know he trusted the people a little more than I did. Even though he trusted them at times, his .45 cal. pistol was always ready to shoot one of them in the head. He did take his pistol out at times. War played tricks on your mind and you had to be ready for anything at all times.

One day when I got back off a patrol around one or two in the afternoon, I went into the building to get out of the sun and to clean my weapons. The Captain of the Popular Forces saw me and started to walk toward me, and he stood in front of me with his .45 cal. pistol, in his hand. The weapon went off and a bullet hit the ground next to my big toe. It was close enough to feel heat on my toe. The round hit the concrete floor and a piece of concrete flew up and hit me in the head. I thought I got a round in my head and fell back on to a folding bed in the corner of the building. At this time four or five Marines that were near me, jumped on the Captain and stated to beat him.

They had him on the ground and were ready to kill him. The Captain started to yell, "Stop, please it was an accident. All I wanted was something to clean my weapon." It was a good thing for him that he said that or he would have been dead. Also I did get up at that time. We didn't worry about paper work if a Vietnamese got shot. He told me he was sorry and asked if I would forgive him. I accepted his apology, but I couldn't really forgive him at that time. I had no feeling of remorse for anything that I had done, so I thought that no one else did either. If I did get shot in the head by accident or by the enemy, tears would still be shed by my family. I couldn't wait to leave this place.

I was with the CAP until the middle of January. One day I went into the village with my brother Jack and walked around for a little while. The people couldn't believe we looked alike, sounded alike, and acted alike. As if we were one person. We always had an interesting time whenever we were together. One thing that never happened was getting shot at when we were in the village together. Jackie did get shot at when he was on watch, around the perimeter of the Air Force Base, in the middle of the night and he was usually on watch every night. We all only had a few hours of sleep each night and put in long days. When we got back to the base camp, they told me I got orders to leave Vietnam. I was happy to be leaving. It is not like I didn't care about the guys I was with. Some guys feel bad about leaving, but not me. I had enough of the jungle and the tension of being on patrol every day, for the last 11 months. I was to leave in a few days. How I left Vietnam is still a mystery to me. I knew I had to go to the Air Force Base, to get on the big beautiful silver bird. I had to give up and check all of my gear and rifle, but I didn't recall doing it. Maybe I had a few drinks to keep me happy.

All I know is that as I walked onto the plane, I stayed between ten Marines also getting out. I didn't want to get shot by a sniper as I was leaving Vietnam. I didn't go near the windows and stayed in the middle of the isle standing until the plane was over water. I then ordered a beer and sat down, and had a few more beers and talked to the girls on the plane. I was not driving so I didn't care if I got drunk. This was the first time since I arrived in Vietnam that I could sit back, and relax.

I was on my way to Okinawa. Good-Bye Vietnam.

CHAPTER 17

OKINAWA

A few hours after boarding a plane and flying out of South Vietnam, I arrived in Okinawa. I was happy to be out of that country with the rain, bugs, rice patties and people shooting at you. After checking in with the Headquarters First Sergeant, the clerk told me that the next day I would be assigned a duty station. I found an empty bed, in the nearest barrack, placed my bags on the floor, and then went into the shower room. For some reason, there were no other Marines around in this barrack. I didn't care if there were anyone around, or where anyone was, I stripped down, and stepped into a warm stream of water. I turned on the water to make it as hot as I could after a few minutes. I had five or six showerheads going towards me at the same time and enjoying every one of them. I stayed in there for an hour. Turning the water from hot to cold, this was the best shower I had in over a year.

I was cleaning Vietnam from my body. I couldn't get enough of this. I put on the clean uniforms that they handed me when I got off the plane. It felt great to be clean again. Any clothes from Vietnam went into the garbage. I wished I could do that with the thoughts in my mind, but those thoughts will be with me forever.

What to do? Anything I wanted until 0800 (8:00 a.m.) the next morning. I took a walk around the base and located the club for the enlisted men. There was a bowling alley and a swimming pool near the barrack where I would be staying. So far, this is turning into a great day. I went to the mess hall, which is open for food almost twenty-four hours a day. I think that they had to close an hour each day to clean up. There were hundreds of Marines going and coming from Vietnam every week. I went to get my plate and one knife, fork, and spoon. I am looking at a steak that just came off the grill and asked the cook if I could have a piece. I nearly broke down and cried when he said to have the whole thing. He then put the steak, sweet potatoes and corn on my plate and said welcome back. The day just got better. I get to eat real food, with real milk, or ice tea, no more Kool-Aid or C-rations. I sat down at a table, ate for an hour and had a big smile on my face when I was finished. I couldn't wait for the morning to come so I could get breakfast.

I went back to the barrack and took a nap. There were no sounds of rifle firing or mortar's in the distance, peaceful sleeping for an hour.

I got up and went to the club for a few beers and to talk to a few guys about what Okinawa was like. I didn't know how long I would be here. I was hoping that they wouldn't send me back to Vietnam. After getting a few burgers and a beer, listening to the music from a live band and enjoying every minute of it, I went back to the barracks and fell asleep. I was up at five the next morning, took a long shower, dressed and put a shine on my new boots. I was the only one in the barrack this morning but I know that won't last for long. I went outside and looked around; no one shooting at me and no mortars were going off in the distance. I was not dreaming. I ran the short distance to the mess hall. They had SOS (shit on a shingle) and I had a smile on my face. I also had a few bacon and eggs sandwiches and a donut along with three cups of coffee.

At 0800, I went to see the First Sergeant for my duty assignment. He said to me, "Do you want to work days or nights?" I said, "Nights would be ok." He said, "Nights it is." You will be the duty NCO, (Non Commission Officer) in charge of liberty, starting at 1630 (4:30 pm) hours and ending at 0800. It will be one day on and two days off. I am listening to all of this and thinking the sergeant is fucking with me. I said, "Am I still in the Marine Corps, sergeant?" I never had a choice for anything in the Marines and didn't think I would have one now.

"That's the way we do things here, corporal, don't get into any trouble on your days off," he replied. I didn't believe this at all and still think that he is fucking with me. He said, "Enjoy the day, and you will start tomorrow at 1630." He got up and walked out of the office. I was in shock, standing there for a few minutes not moving.

I started to smile and said, "What the fuck, it seems to be real."

I went back to the mess hall and had something more to eat. After eating, I went to the PX (Post Exchange, which is a retail store on the base, a general store where personal items could be bought—cigarettes, shaving items, etc.) and picked up a newspaper and another cup of coffee. I found a medium size bathing suit, paid a few dollars for it and headed for the pool to think about what just happened. I had a big smile on my face and said to myself, this is going to turn out to be a good place if this was for real. I have to be careful not to fuck this up.

Welcome to Camp Hanson, Okinawa.

After swimming and taking it easy all day, I went to the club after I had a few steaks at the mess hall. I stayed in the club until two in the morning; had a few beers, listened to the music and had something more to eat. The food was much better than C-Rations. I didn't see any girls yet in the club, maybe on the weekend.

I returned to the barracks and there were a couple of guys that just got in this morning. One guy was a little drunk and asked me if I needed any weapons. I said, "No, I left all of my weapons in the Nam." He opened his locker and it was filled with rifles and pistols.

He said, "You can buy anything you want from him." "Thanks anyway," I said and would let him know the next day.

The next morning after breakfast, I was thinking that these guys could fuck up a good thing for me being in the same barracks. It would be only a matter of time before these Marines got drunk and started to shoot, at unknown shadows. That did happen often to guys who just left the Nam. I was not sure if my plan would work, but I went over to the First Sergeant and asked him if I could change my sleeping location, so that I would be closer to headquarters, in case there were any problems I could help. He said that was a great idea and I could move into the barrack at the far end of the headquarters building. He said pick any bunk you want, before the new troops get here in a few days. He said, "Don't worry; no one will be dropping any mortars on us." I said thanks, I felt more comfortable in an area where I may be needed. Since I didn't start my new job until later in the day, I went back to the barracks and got all my things. The two new guys were just getting up, and I told them that I have to move out because the fucking lifer sergeant wanted me closer to where I had to work. They started to laugh and said good luck. A week later, they were both locked up for selling weapons on the black market. Don't know who told on them, but I was happy. I also thought about getting hit by bullets, if these idiots started to shoot at each other in the middle of the night.

The first day of duty involved checking ID cards and giving out liberty passes. The line starts at 1630 (4:30 p.m.) hours and by 2000 (8:00 p.m.), everything was quiet and I could sit back and read a book. This life gets better every day. There were a few guys who didn't have liberty passes, most of them were cooks, and would beg me to let them go out for a couple of hours. I said ok to most of them. Since the guys were cooks from the mess hall, they said whatever I wanted I could get without waiting on line. I found out that when there were Marines coming from the Nam, or the states at the same time, the lines were long. I never waited for food. Some nights they would bring me bacon and eggs or steaks. One night I wanted a glass of milk and asked a cook that was just getting back off liberty for some. He had someone drop off a five-gallon container. What the fuck am I going to do with that? I had a few glasses, and then gave the rest of it away.

I found out that I would be in Camp Hanson for almost two months. I needed this time of happiness to make up for the last year.

There were a few incidents that I had to take care of while on duty late at night. The mugging of an officer was the first one. The Marines that did the mugging were seen running back to the base. I had to go into every barrack, wake all the Marines and have them stand in front of their bunks. Many of them said "Go fuck yourself," which I would have said just coming back from the Nam. I didn't want to do this, but the duty officer said to do it. This went on for a couple of hours, and the officer that got mugged walked in front of each Marine. He didn't find the ones who mugged him. I said it may have been an officer, and that we should check the Officers' Quarters. That didn't get over to well, and then the sun started to pop out. This time the officers were safe.

Towards the end of my visit to Camp Hanson, a private got attacked by two officers in the town just outside the front gates. I decided to wake up all the officers. I was going back to the States in a couple of weeks, what the fuck, give them hell Jerry. I had the MP'S with me and had each officer stand in front of the private. He said he didn't see the officers who did this to him. I think he waited to find the officers in town, a few nights later and smacked them around. There were no charges against anyone.

Every morning after my duty, I would go to the pool and swim for a little while. I would then jog to the gym and punch the heavy bag for an hour. After a shower, I headed for the mess hall where I would eat for an hour, read a book and have a few cups of coffee. A great job and duty station as long as I didn't have to go back to Vietnam.

One morning I went to the bowling alley and saw someone I knew from the states. I got him a beer and we started a game. He told me he was stationed on this base.

He had nine straight strikes, going for a perfect score. While we waited for his last ball to return, four MP'S came over and locked him up. He was UA, (un-authorized absent.) They have been watching him for a few weeks, going on and off the base, and decided to get him that morning. I don't remember the reason they wanted him, but he did go to jail for a couple of years. Thousands of guys coming into the base each week can't be all as good as me.

The week before I was to leave Okinawa, I was going into the disbursement office to get paid and started to talk to a guy who said he knew a few guys that served with me in the states. He started to walk ahead of me and said hello to the MP'S as he entered the office. As his money was handed to him, an officer said, "Wait, don't give him anything." With that, the Marine grabbed a large metal ashtray from the counter, smashed the Lieutenant in the face with it, and ran out of the room. He pushed me into the MP 'S as he was running out and got off the base before getting caught. Because I was with him, they questioned me, and wanted to know where this guy lived in the town. I said I couldn't know that if I just met him going into the building. After a few minutes of questioning, they let me go. That night while on duty the MP'S brought a prisoner in and said someone had to watch him. "Not me," I said. This was the guy that hit the officer. Someone walked in and said he would watch him in the barrack across the field, and kicked the prisoner in the stomach as hard as he could and then said, "You are a dirt bag" and kicked him again. The MP'S liked that and said, "Ok." The prisoner was handcuffed to a steal beam with his hands behind his back. The next morning the prisoner was gone and the guard that kicked him the day before was knocked out on the floor. It turned out that the guard grew up with him and they were best friends for years. He let him go. They both were caught years later in town doing something wrong.

As the days were coming close for me to leave, I did a few stupid things, like getting my hair cut in a style not allowed by the Marine Corps. I had to shave my head before getting my orders to leave as a punishment.

I went into town a couple of days before leaving and ordered two or three sharkskin suits and five silk shirts all tailored made. I had them sent to New York.

On the last night of duty, I played a song by the Righteous Brothers for reveille, at five thirty in the morning to awaken the camp. I lied and said that the switch for the loud speaker was stuck in the on position. They didn't believe me but couldn't prove that it wasn't. I thought that it would be a funny thing to do but the officers didn't like it. "Too fucking bad for them if they can't take a joke."

I was to leave the next morning to go back to the United States; I couldn't wait. I had enough of the Far East and wanted to go back to American girls and my family. With my new suits and shirts waiting for me at home, I will be ready to have a good time.

CHAPTER 18

BACK IN THE UNITE STATES OF AMERICA

In April 1967, I returned to the United States, after more than a year in Vietnam and Okinawa it was great to be back. I only had a few more months left until September to get my discharge from the Marine Corps. All the hardships and pains of a combat tour were over and now, I can be back in America, where people would like and respect you.

After the plane landed on the military base, I got my leave papers and my new duty station assignment after a few hours of doing paper work. I then headed to the Los Angeles Airport, in California for a well-deserved vacation, thirty days of fun-time. I was with a few friends that I knew and they were also returning home. We sat in the terminal bar and we all ordered a beer. Some of the guys had to get an earlier plane to their hometown, so we all wanted to say our goodbyes. As we were drinking the beer one guy pulled out a pistol, which he got from the battlegrounds off a dead VC soldier that he shot. It was a small, but nice pistol and after looking at it, we left it in the corner of the table. After ten minutes, the bar keeper came over to us and said, "Guys, that can't stay out on the table."

We all looked at the table, and said, "What?" He pointed at the pistol and we realized what he was talking about. All the other people in the bar that were having drinks or food ran out.

We carried our weapons every day for a year and didn't think anything of this. We are back in the world. For some of us, it was from the battlegrounds to the airport. Two of the Marines with me, were in the middle of the jungle, fighting every day for over a year. They left the jungles of Vietnam and came right to California. After an hour of drinking they went to their gate, boarded their plane and I went with the other two guys, to a restaurant inside the airport to eat. We had a couple of hours before my flight left for New York.

I don't know how I got away with what happened next, but I did. Before sitting down, standing next to a seat in the restaurant, five young men walked by me and the other Marines and each one of them banged into me and said, "Fuck you."

I said, "Excuse me for being in your fucking way, you fucking scumbags." One of the guys had some remarks to make about the military and they started to walk back toward us. I reached down into the bag, which my fellow Marine had and found the pistol we had on the table. I grabbed the first guy that came close to me, put the pistol to his face and said, "Maybe you would want a bullet in your fucking head." Sweat poured out of him, as if someone just threw a glass of water in his face. He said he was sorry. No shit, what else would you say if you had a weapon in your face? I told them to get out of the fucking restaurant, then sat down and ate. No one else said anything, to our surprise and no cops came in. The pistol had to be checked at the gate, before my friend boarded the plane. The security was not like it is today. They told him that they would give the gun back after the plane landed.

I couldn't believe the attitude of some people. We had put our lives on the line for our country for over a year. My brother Jackie was still over there and my brother Dennis got shot up and was put into a hospital for a few months. No one gave a fuck. It seemed like the only person who changed was me. Everyone was enjoying the good life back in the United States and didn't care about the warriors, mentally or physically wounded returning home from a war. The hardships of war stayed in Vietnam and in the back of our minds for now.

I was happy to be flying out of California and heading toward John F Kennedy airport, in New York. It has been over a year since my last leave and I am putting Vietnam out of my mind while going to New York.

The plane landed at Kennedy with no problems, no one shooting at us, a safe landing. I grabbed my sea-bag from the luggage area and stepped outside in the fresh cool night breeze to get a taxi home. I had my uniform on and I was proud to be a Marine.

I waited outside the terminal for a taxi. Three or four taxi's pulled up to me and then pulled away before I could get in. It was two in the morning. I waited for the next taxi to slow down in front of me and grabbed the door, opened it then jumped in. The driver said he doesn't take military people, he doesn't like us. "Get out of my cab," he said. I don't remember everything that night, but I did have a knife in my pocket, which I took out and placed it on his neck. I screamed, "Get me the fuck out of here or I will cut your fucking throat!" I told him to drive toward Brooklyn on the parkway. When I was about a mile from the airport (I thought I could go to jail for this), I told him to stop the car and gave him some money for the fare.

I got out and said, "Don't stop driving, keep going to Brooklyn." I started to run the couple of miles to my house. I ran across the parkway, down the side streets, empty lots and train tracks near my parent's house. Before going near the house, I waited in the weeds that are a block away, looked around and made sure no cops were driving by looking for me. I finally went to the house. I don't know if the driver told the police what happened, but I hoped that the police told him to shut up and keep driving. The taxi driver should have been put in jail, or maybe hell.

Welcome to New York City.

I was not the only one returning home that year and being shit on by people who felt that all Marines were baby killers. Thankfully that attitude and thinking has changed today, maybe because of the number of books that were written about the hardships of war and the way Vietnam Veterans were treated when they came home from an unpopular war. During War World Two, the military dropped many bombs on cities and the biggest bombs at the end. I am sure there were many children killed at that time, but we didn't hear that the soldiers were baby killers. "Don't condemn the warrior for doing his job."

Everyone was happy that I got home safe. My mother wanted to know what Jackie was doing and if he was near the shooting or any unsafe places. I told my mother and father that he had a party every night, drinking and dancing with the nurses and any other American girls he could find. "He may even marry a Vietnamese girl," I said with a laugh. But really, he could have been killed any night or day that he was in Vietnam, by mortars or booby traps. I prayed that night as I had many others that he got home safe. The lie made my mother happy and she probably slept better that night than she did all year.

My uniform stayed in the closet for the next thirty days. I didn't feel like defending my actions in a war zone to anyone who has been sitting on their ass in the world of freedom while I was getting shot at.

Some friends and neighbors that I spoke to thought that I died in Vietnam. "I didn't see you around, so we thought you died," they said. "Thanks for thinking about me," I said. In Vietnam, there are no phones and even my parents didn't know sometimes for months if I were alive, dead or wounded in a hospital. Mail didn't come every day. We couldn't write letters that often in the jungle. When we did write letters, it would take weeks for someone to send them back to the battalion area for delivery to the states.

I went to Manhattan on the weekend with my two brothers and a few friends to German town on the Upper East Side. I went to the Irish bars and dance halls Jackie and I used to go to before Vietnam. I didn't worry about the people or the area that I was in; as long as I wasn't in the jungle, I had a good time. Some nights we would go our separate ways in the city. I would walk around, go to an all-night coffee shop and then walked down some of the streets in the city that I should not be on. Maybe inside I wanted to fight, I felt like I wanted to do something exciting. I was at a loss. Deep down in my mind maybe I needed the excitement of the jungle or to have other Marines with me. The feeling was with me for years and it always came back.

My leave time came to an end quickly, thirty days is not long to be home. But I had to go back to Camp Lejeune, North Carolina. I went by bus from 42nd street in Manhattan. I think my brother Dennis dropped me off at the terminal on 8th Avenue. He said he would take a ride down to visit me. He just came back from Vietnam a year earlier. He knew what I was going through.

Only a few more months at Camp Lejeune and I will be getting out of the Marines. I didn't have to carry a rifle around with me; no one was shooting at me on base. The Marines assigned me to a Tank Battalion for the next four or five months. It was a great duty station. No one told me what to do and usually I did what I wanted. The Captain of the company wasn't a lifer and also wanted his time off. Any time it looked like rain, he would say, "Do not bring the tanks out of the garage." If the tanks got dirty, we would have to clean the outside of the tanks with a steel brush and the captain would have to inspect them. He didn't want to do that. The Marine Corps didn't like dirt.

We did have to take the tanks out for a ride thought the woods every couple of weeks. One day a black sergeant asked me if I ever drove a tank, I said, "Of course I had." I felt that I couldn't get hurt inside a tank and everything in front of me would be knocked down. I did not care. I went as fast as I could up and down the hills, to me it was a joy ride. The sergeant didn't like it, yelled for me to stop, and stood in front of the tank. It was stupid on his part because I didn't really know how to stop it. When I went forward I gave it too much gas and nearly ran him over. He was pissed and ran over to me when I got out of the tank and started to wave his finger in my face and screaming, "You fucking jerk!" I grabbed his finger and almost broke it, I told him to shut the fuck up and leave me alone. He never talked to me again for the next four months. I guess he couldn't take a joke. No one else from my tank platoon had gone to Vietnam yet, so I think no one wanted to piss me off. I didn't think there was anything wrong with me. The captain asked me a couple of times if I wanted to ship over, but I said, "No, I don't think so," to signing up for another four years. I did my time in hell.

CHAPTER 19

DISCHARGE FROM THE MARINE CORPS

My departure from the Marines was coming soon. In fact, it was only a week away. I had to watch what I said to everyone who had a higher rank than I did. I needed some of the Sergeants to sign my papers saying that I returned all of the military gear that was given to me, when I arrived at Camp Lejeune, North Carolina, six months ago. I also had to have someone from the base barbershop, sign my papers stating that my hair wasn't long. Leaving the Marine Corps after four years wasn't hard at all for me in September 1967. At 21 years old and four years active service with the Marines, I had seen the good side and the bad of many countries in the world. I had experienced the pain and hardship of going to war and also seen those who are now the walking dead. I wanted to move on with my life. I didn't know what I wanted now, but I knew that the Marine Corps were not in my plans. I didn't want to take orders from the lifers that stayed in with the Marines for years. The long years in the Marine Corps taking orders from everyone wasn't for me, I didn't have anything against anyone who stayed in. (Lifers are those that stayed in the service for over twenty years.) After checking out and saying my good byes and promising to keep in touch with everyone, I walked to the bus terminal. This was my second good-bye to a group of men that I served with. I spent my time in hell, now it is time to get out.

I boarded a bus, in Jacksonville, North Carolina, and headed toward New York City. This time going through the southern states was much different from four years ago. Blacks were now drinking and eating at the same counter.

I remembered in 1964 when I was going to New York City from North Carolina by bus, I had stopped in some cities on the way to get something to eat. I went to the counter and ordered a couple of burgers and a milk shake. I was told that I couldn't be served on this side of the bus terminal. I was in the Marine Corps, just out of boot camp and was told I couldn't eat on this side of the restaurant. I told everyone to go fuck themselves and give me my fucking food. There was no reason for me to go anywhere else, I was a fucking Marine and I wanted to eat. A cop came over to me and said, "Whites don't eat with the blacks." The other side of the terminal had better food. "Don't cause any trouble and go to the other side."

That was the first time that I ran across something like this. In New York, we didn't have that type of separation. True there were areas that only blacks or whites lived in, but they were allowed to walk on the same side of the street as whites. I went to high school with blacks, in many of my classes. I never had any problems with them. I went to the other side of the building. My only concern at this time was eating. I didn't care about the blacks or whites from the south. I turned and left a run down, dirty looking, dilapidated place, with one low wattage light bulb above the counter top and walked a few feet away, to a place that looked like a night club. Bright lights all around the room and music that was playing, the latest hits from the jukebox in the corner, a very clean and nice place. I guess whites do have it better down here in the south.

Blacks were permitted in the theater to see the movies but had to sit up in the balcony; they were allowed to do that only in some sections of the cities. I went with a couple of Marines one day to the theater in North Carolina and we were told to sit in the lower level of the movie house. I said bullshit I wanted to sit up in the balcony because it was 25 cents cheaper. In New York City, the balcony had the better seats. I said I wanted to be charged for the balcony and that is where I am going. The other guys grabbed me and pushed me to the lower level near the back row. I said, "There is no good reason to sit down here instead of the balcony, loud enough for the whole place to hear."

At that time four big men with loud Southern accents stood up, in the front row of the theater and said, "Where is that black lover that wants to go up into the balcony with the blacks." The guys with me said if I were to open my mouth, they would kill me. I did keep quiet. People in the south in the 60's didn't care too much for Catholics or New Yorkers at that time either.

Traveling to New York four years later, the south did change. I had my Sea-bag, which had all my military uniforms, new civilian clothes, and a few personnel items to take home with me. I had money in my pockets and savings in the bank, I could do anything. But what, should I do?

My twin brother Jackie was already home. The Marines discharged him about two months before me. When he left Vietnam he only had a few months left of service life, so the Marines said "We had enough of you get out". When he was in California, waiting for his papers to be discharged, he decided to go for a ride up the coast. The only problem he had at that time was that he didn't own a car. So, he took a jeep, from the motor pool when no one was looking. He was having a great time. He forgot that the jeep he took from the motor pool didn't belong to him. He used it until he ran out of gas. The MP'S found him drunk in Hollywood, sleeping on the back seat of the jeep. For some reason, he had talked his way out of jail. The commanding officer handed him his discharge paper, when he returned to base and said to him, "Get the fuck out of my Marine Corps." If you were not just back from Vietnam, I would put your fucking ass in jail. Jack said, "Yes Sir," turned and walked away with a big smile on his face. He always got away with many things that would have put others in jail.

I was home for only a couple of days and wanted to do something. I always wanted to go to college, so I jumped on a train, went downtown to New York University and asked for information to enroll. The campus was large and the information that they gave me was over bearing. I was intimidated. Four years in the Marines and I was intimidated. I took the information home with me and told my parents and Jackie. "Why bother going to school?" they asked. "Move on and get a job." I was not a great student in high school, before joining the Marines so I moved on, a mistake that I had to live with for many years. (I did go back to school years later and received a degree in applied science. I was the only one in my family to go to college. I still have a desire to learn more.)

I wanted a job. Sitting around, hanging out was not for me. I told Jackie to get up off his fucking ass and come with me. We went to the main office of many of the construction trades, in New York City and filled out applications for employment. They all said, "We will get in touch with you, have a nice day." On the way home, we stopped in all the bars on 3rd Avenue for a drink. We got home around two in the morning and got up at five. Jackie and I got on the train again to Manhattan looking for a job. We stopped in a coffee house, for some pancakes and eggs in midtown, before going to an employment center. Jackie took a job in a print shop with a large firm near Wall Street. We had no experience, so we took the first job that was offered to us. I started the next day in a bank, a few blocks from where Jackie was going to work. It was a large bank downtown New York City. While waiting to be interviewed and to fill out papers, a girl walked in, and sat down, in the waiting room. I offered to buy her a cup of coffee. We talked for five minutes and then I left. The bank had a large lunchroom and all you could eat for free. This was a good start for me. After a week, I knew that this job was not for me. I told the boss to transfer me to the printing department or maybe even the computer department. He said, "Ok, after Christmas." The holidays were only two months away and I didn't want to spend any of the money that I saved, so I worked doing what I didn't want to do. While in the lunchroom, I started to talk to a few of the girls around me. I asked a couple of them out for drinks, or to the movies. The looks I got from them were looks of hate. I couldn't believe it. None of the girls were talking to me and after all those looks, I wanted to know why.

One girl walked by me, as I was leaving the cafeteria and said to me, "I don't know how you could do that to Jane, it is wrong she loves you so much."

I said, "I don't know anyone by the name of Jane." It turned out that Jane was the girl that I got coffee for on that first day, so in Jane's mind she thought that I loved her and she told everyone that we were going to be married. I told everyone what a screwed up woman she was and I hoped that she would leave the company. I did go out with a few of the girls after they realized how nice I was. Lesson learned. Don't buy coffee for nut-jobs.

Before New Year's Day, January 1, the bank needed to get accounts out and the boss asked me to work on New Year's Eve. I told him that morning that I would work.

During the day I asked about my transfer to a different department, he said, "No, You will be staying here with me." When 5:00 P.M. came around, everyone else from the office, left to enjoy New Year's Eve. I waited until 5:30 P.M. and told the boss that I was going home, to enjoy the New Year. He said, "You can't go, you told me, that you were going to work tonight."

I said, "You are right, but you told me I would be transferred to another department, so go fuck yourself." I quit and walked out. It was New Year's Eve, so I went to a local bar with some of the guys that I knew from the Neighborhood. I could not find any girls by themselves so I went home. A few days later, I packed up my clothes in a small suitcase and went to Florida.

I did sign up for the unemployment money before deciding to go to Florida, $52 dollars a week for 26 weeks. I could live on that for now. I traveled to Vietnam, and many other places with the Marines, so to travel a few miles south, did not stop me. I boarded a plane and was down in South Beach, Miami, Florida in three hours.

My brother Dennis met me at the airport. He was living in South Beach, in a hotel near the water. I said this was great, I could be happy down here. I got a room near the beach in a small hotel. It was cold and only 10 degrees when I left New York City. It was 80 degrees now in Florida, at 12:30 in the morning and it felt great. How can anyone not like this place? I dropped off my suitcase and said to Dennis, "It is time to eat." To my surprise, my brother David was waiting for us, at the coffee shop with some of his friends. I learned later that they all were beach bums, looking for someone to help them out with a few dollars. I wasn't going to fall into David's trap of being his banker. He tried to do that many times to me when he was living in New York. He had a way with words and would try to make everyone feel sorry for him. He would say, "You are working and I am not, please help me out, I am your oldest brother." The problem with David was that he never wanted to work. He was a con artist, but smart enough to get any job he applied for, if he wanted to work. I did buy everyone breakfast. I am in the sunshine state, warm without an overcoat on and was glad to see everyone. This buying for everyone wasn't going to happen every day. I saved my money and I expect everyone to do the same. After eating, it was around three o'clock in the morning and still 80 degree's. I told Dennis, that I am going to jump into the ocean now and go for a swim. He took me to the beach and returned to his hotel for some sleep. After swimming, I walked back to my hotel and slept for two hours. I got up at 6:00 a.m. to have pancakes on the beach.

This was a great place and I had fun. There were a few problems with the local police. The problem was with them, not me. The third day I got up a few minutes earlier to go to the beach to go swimming and have a long walk in the sand before eating. I had a towel around my neck, sandals on my feet and a bathing suit on. A patrol car pulls up on the sidewalk in front of me and a cop jumps out and said, "Let me see some ID." I told him my ID was back in my room at the hotel. I still had my military ID. He said, walk back to the hotel and I will meet you there. He drove a few feet behind me watching that I didn't run. He wanted to come up to my room, so I told the building manager and his assistant to come with me. The cop didn't like that.

"They can stay down stairs and I will go up with you," said the officer.

I said, "No, they have to come with me." In the room, he asked me what I was doing in Florida. I said, I just came out of the Marine Corps and told him that I will be working with Captain James tomorrow morning and will be on the

Dade County Police Department. I didn't know Captain James, but someone said, months before to use his name if any cops in Dade County fucks with you. The cop started to shake, said he was sorry and would take me back to the beach. He said, "Say hello to Captain James for me," and drove the car right up on to the sand and opened the door of the car for me.

"I will go fuck with some colored folks," he said. I never found out who the captain was that I was such good friends with.

I enjoyed the next few months on the beach every morning, working out in the 5th street gym with different prize fighters in the afternoon and going to the night spots every night to dance. One day in the gym, a fighter said to jump in the ring and do some sparing with him. I said, "Ok I won't hurt you."

I punched him as hard as I could for five minutes and he stood there with his hands down and said, "Is that the best that you have?"

I said, "Fuck you" and got out of the ring. Boxing was not for me. I enjoyed the physical action of the sport but the training is intense. I guess that is why most fighters put on many extra pounds after their career ends and they don't have to train as hard. I said to the guy that it is easier to use a gun if someone fucks with me.

I ate out two or three times a day, lived a block away from the water in a decent hotel and enjoyed the nightlife, all on the $52 dollars a week, that I got from the New York State

Unemployment Office. In New York City I worked for $75 dollars a week, in Florida I am having a great time on $52 dollars a week.

I would get my checks twice a month for $104 dollars each and cash them in the local bank. One day there was a cute looking teller at the window and as I handed her my check, I asked her for a date. She looked at my check, which had New York Unemployment printed on it and said, "Fuck you." She was only making $60 dollars a week. I guess her thoughts were that I made $104 a week, sitting on my ass and enjoying the beach. She missed an opportunity. As they say, there are many fish in the sea.

I stayed in Florida until April 2, 1968. I got called for a job installing elevators with the Local One Elevator Union, on new construction sites in Manhattan, New York. I was to start on April 9, 1968. I had to get transportation to New York and didn't want to go by bus. My friend, who lived in Maryland, said he would drive to New York with me and get a bus from there to go home. I found a place that needed drivers to drive cars to all parts of the United States. I would get paid a few dollars to drive the car, plus money for tolls and gas. I got five days to drop the car off on Long Island to a private home. We took turns driving and got to New York in 24 hours. We also got two speeding tickets, speed traps, one in Georgia the other in New Jersey.

We dropped the car off early on the morning of April 4, 1968. My friend said he would be going home today, so from Howard Beach we took the "A" train into Manhattan and then walked around the upper eastside for a few hours.

We had lunch and started to walk west on 42nd Street, to the bus terminal. It was getting dark around 7 p.m. As we walked toward the west side, there were many people in the street near Times Square yelling, "Fuck the whites." My friend said (being a southerner), "Let's go beat the shit out of those blacks."

I said, "Let's get the fuck out of here, we are outnumbered" as I grabbed his arm and started to walk downtown a few blocks and then walked west over to the bus station, using 38th street.

I watched him get on the bus then turned toward the exit to look for a taxi. The driver of the yellow cab pulled up and said, "Where are you going?"

I said, "Queens, the other side of the 59th street Bridge."

"Good," he said. "Let's get the fuck out of the city." He didn't charge me when we got to Woodside, so I got him a beer and said be careful. He didn't want to be near a black neighborhood that night.

Martin Luther King was shot and killed around 6:00 p.m. on April 4, 1968. People said it was James Earl Ray that fired the deadly shot. Like the many assassination conspiracy theories on who killed John F Kennedy, Martin L. King would have just as many theories as the years went by.

What we know for sure is that hate killed the King.

I got home safe that night and enjoyed a few days with my family, then started my new career installing elevators on April 9, 1968. Jackie and I were now back together, living in our family home and leaving for work each day to our jobs in New York City. We went about our lives doing many of the same things we did before we left home for boot camp at age 17. Eventually we had our own families and didn't always speak about those experiences with them.

When we returned home from the Marines, my brother Jackie and I were under the impression that our lives would be back to normal after we returned home from Vietnam. We hardly spoke of the hardships we endured in the hopes that if we didn't speak about it, it would just go away. However, over the years, I came to understand the overwhelming impact those four years had and continue to have on my life. Only my brothers in arms, who served their country in Vietnam, know firsthand that—life would never be the same.

Jerry Byrne

THE OTHER BATTLE

By Jerry Byrne

A HARD LIFE OF

BATTLES AND FEAR

THE END OF LIFE'S LOAN

IS FINALLY HERE

INTO THE BUNKER WITH

SWEAT AND TEARS

HE FOUGHT OFF THE ENEMY

HE KNEW FOR YEARS

THEY WILL NOT TAKE ME ALIVE

HE HAD SAID MANY TIMES

MEMORY OF HIS FAMILY ON HIS MIND

THE HEART BROKE AND THE SHAKES

WERE GONE

DROPPED INTO DARKNESS FOR ALL TIMES

THE CHILDREN'S TEARS STARTED TO FLOW

THEIR DADDY'S EYES

WERE CLOSED

POST TRAUMATIC STRESS

TOOK ITS TOLL

THE ENEMY RETURNS

By Jerry Byrne

AS THE SUN MOVES

TOWARDS THE OCEAN DEEP

SHADOWS OF THE NIGHT

START TO CREEP

THE BODY ACHING

TO STAY AWAKE

WAS THAT MOVEMENT NEAR THE GATE

WHAT ONCE WAS A STRANGE LOOKING TREE

NOW HAS ARMS AND LEGS AND TEETH

EYES WET WITH SWEAT

HANDS STARTED TO SHAKE

CIRCLES OF DARKNESS

SOON TO BE

THE BATTLE IS OVER

PEACE ALL AROUND

POST TRAUMATIC STRESS

CAN NOT BE FOUND

BENEATH THE GROUND

ABOUT THE AUTHOR

Jerry Byrne is a Combat Vietnam Veteran. He retired from the elevator industry after 35 years of service. Jerry is active in a variety of veterans' organizations. Jerry is a frequent guest speaker at high schools throughout Long Island, New York where he speaks to students, about his Vietnam experience.

There are thousands of books written about Vietnam but not necessarily about twins in boot camp and Vietnam at the same time. This book is history, but it's not a history book. It is a story written as I remembered Vietnam and the hardship of being a grunt in the Marine Corps. The story highlights growing up as twins in New York City and joining the Marine Corps together.

My brother, John's life was taken away at the early age of 58. He died from Agent Orange, a toxic chemical produced by greedy corporations. Many Americans were exposed to this while fighting in Vietnam and are still dying from it today.

Twin Marines in Hell: From Grade School to Vietnam